Dragonswan

Sherrilyn Kenyon

D0037338

JOVE BOOKS, NEW YORK

THE BERKLEY PUBLISHING GROUP
Published by the Penguin Group
Penguin Group (USA) Inc.
375 Hudson Street, New York, New York 10014, USA
Penguin Group (Canada), 90 Eglinton Avenue East, Suite 700, Toronto, Ontario M4P 2Y3, Canada
(a division of Pearson Penguin Canada Inc.)
Penguin Books Ltd., 80 Strand, London WC2R 0RL, England
Penguin Group Ireland, 25 St. Stephen's Green, Dublin 2, Ireland (a division of Penguin Books Ltd.)
Penguin Group (Australia), 250 Camberwell Road, Camberwell, Victoria 3124, Australia
(a division of Pearson Australia Group Pty. Ltd.)
Penguin Books India Pvt. Ltd., 11 Community Centre, Panchsheel Park, New Delhi—110 017, India
Penguin Group (NZ), Cnr. Airborne and Rosedale Roads, Albany, Auckland 1310, New Zealand
(a division of Pearson New Zealand Ltd.)
Penguin Books (South Africa) (Pty.) Ltd., 24 Sturdee Avenue, Rosebank, Johannesburg 2196,
South Africa

Penguin Books Ltd., Registered Offices: 80 Strand, London WC2R 0RL, England

This is a work of fiction. Names, characters, places, and incidents either are the product of the author's imagination or are used fictitiously, and any resemblance to actual persons, living or dead, business establishments, events, or locales is entirely coincidental.

DRAGONSWAN

A Jove Book / published by arrangement with the author

PRINTING HISTORY
Jove mass-market edition / September 2005

"Dragonswan" was previously included as a short story in *Tapestry* published by Jove in September 2002.

ISBN: 0-515-14079-1

JOVE®
Jove Books are published by The Berkley Publishing Group,
a division of Penguin Group (USA) Inc.,
375 Hudson Street, New York, New York 10014.
JOVE is a registered trademark of Penguin Group (USA) Inc.
The "J" design is a trademark belonging to Penguin Group (USA) Inc.

PRINTED IN THE UNITED STATES OF AMERICA

10 9 8 7 6 5 4 3 2 1

Dragonswan

One

"Be kind to dragons, for thou art crunchy when roasted and taste good with ketchup."

Dr. Channon MacRae paused in her note-taking and arched a brow at the peculiar comment. She'd been staring at the famous Dragon Tapestry for hours, trying to decipher the Old English symbolism, and in all this time no one had disturbed her.

Not until now.

With her most irritated look, she pulled her pen away from her notepad and turned.

Then she gaped.

No annoying, irreverent little man here. He was a tall, mind-blowingly sexy god who dominated the small museum room with a presence so powerful that she wondered how on earth he had entered the building without shaking it to its foundations.

Never in her life had she beheld anything like him or the seductive smile he flashed at her.

Good grief, she couldn't take her eyes off him.

Standing at least six feet five, he towered over her average height. His long black hair was pulled back into a sleek ponytail, and he wore an expensively tailored black suit and overcoat that seemed at odds with his unorthodox hair yet perfectly fitting with his regal aura.

But the most peculiar thing of all was the tattoo covering the left half of his face. A faded dark green, it spiraled and curled from his hairline to his chin like some ancient symbol.

On anyone else such a mark would be freakish or strange, but this man wore it with dignity and presence— like a proud birthright.

Yet it was his eyes that captivated her most. A rich, deep, greenish-gold, they were filled with such warm intelligence and vitality that it left her completely breathless.

His grin was both boyish and roguish and framed by inviting dimples that enchanted her. "Rendered you speechless, eh?"

She loved the sound of his voice, which was laced with an accent she couldn't quite place. It seemed a unique blending of the British and Greek. Not to mention, deep and provocative.

"Not quite speechless," she said, resisting the urge to smile back at him. "I'm just wondering why you would say such a thing."

He shrugged his broad shoulders nonchalantly as his golden gaze dropped to her lips, making her want to lick them. Worse, his prolonged stare sent a rush of desire coiling though her.

Suddenly, it was so extremely warm in this little glass room that she half expected the gallery windows to fog up.

He folded his hands casually behind his back, yet he seemed coiled for action, as if he were ready and alert to take on anyone who threatened him.

What a strange image to have . . .

When he spoke again, his deep voice was even more seductive and enticing than it had been before, almost as if it were weaving some kind of magical spell around her. "You had such a serious frown while you were staring at the tapestry that it made me wonder what you would look like with a smile in its place."

Oh, the man was beguiling. And just a little too cocksure of his appeal, judging by his arrogant stance. No doubt he could get any woman who caught his eye.

Channon swallowed at the thought as she glanced down at her tan corduroy jumper and her hips, which were not the fashionable, narrow kind. She'd never been the type of woman who drew the notice of a man like this. She'd been lucky if her average looks ever garnered her a second glance at all.

Mr. Do-Me-Right-Now must have lost a bet or something. Why else would he be speaking to her?

Still, there was an air of danger, intrigue, and power about him. But none of deceit. He appeared honest and, strangely enough, interested in her.

How could that be?

"Yes, well," she said, taking a step to her left as she closed her pad and slid her pen down the spiral coil, "I don't make it my habit to converse with strangers, so if you'll excuse me . . ."

"Sebastian."

Startled by his response, she paused and looked up. "What?"

"My name is Sebastian." He held his hand out to her. "Sebastian Kattalakis. And you are?"

Completely stunned and amazed that you're talking to me.

She blinked the thought away. "Channon," she said before she could stop herself. "Shannon with a C."

His gaze burned her while a small smile hovered at the edges of those well-shaped lips and he flashed the tiniest bit of his dimples. There was an indescribable masculine aura about him that seemed to say he would be far more at home on some ancient battlefield than locked inside this museum.

He took her cold hand into his large, warm one. "So very pleased to meet you, Shannon with a C."

He kissed her knuckles like some gallant knight of long ago. Her heart pounded at the feel of his hot breath against her skin, of his warm lips on her flesh. It was all she could do not to moan from the sheer pleasure of it.

No man had ever treated her this way—like some treasured lady to be quested for.

She felt oddly beautiful around him. Desirable.

"Tell me, Channon," he said, releasing her hand and glancing from her to the tapestry. "What has you so interested in this?"

Channon looked back at it and the intricate embroidery that covered the yellowed linen. Honestly, she didn't know. Since she'd first seen it as a little girl, she'd been in love with this ancient masterpiece. She'd spent years studying the detailed dragon fable that started with the birth of a male infant and a dragon and moved forward through ten feet of fabric.

Scholars had written countless papers on their theories of its origin. She, herself, had done her dissertation on it, trying to link it to the tales of King Arthur or to Celtic tradition.

No one knew where the tapestry had come from or even what story it related to. For that matter, no one knew who had won the fight between the dragon and the warrior.

That was what intrigued her most of all.

"I wish I knew how it ended."

He flexed his jaw. "The story has no ending. The battle between the dragon and the man lives on unto today."

She frowned at him. He appeared serious. "You think so?"

"What?" he asked good-naturedly. "You don't believe me?"

"Let's just say I have a hefty dose of doubt."

He took a step forward, and again his fierce, manly presence overwhelmed her and sent a jolt of desire through her. "Hmmm, a hefty dose of doubt," he said, his voice barely more than a low, deep growl. "I wonder what I could do to make you believe?"

She should step back, she knew it. Yet she couldn't make her feet cooperate. His clean, spicy scent invaded her head and weakened her knees.

What was it about this man that made her want to stand here talking to him?

Oh, to heck with that. What she really wanted to do was jump his delectable bones. To cup that handsome face of his in her hands and kiss his lips until she was drunk from his taste.

There was something seriously wrong here.

Mayday. Mayday.

"Why are you here?" she asked, trying to keep her lecherous thoughts at bay. "You hardly look like the type to study medieval relics."

A wicked gleam came into his eyes. "I'm here to steal it."

She scoffed at the idea, even though something inside her said it wouldn't be too much of a stretch to buy that explanation. "Are you really?"

"Of course. Why else would I be here?"

"Why else, indeed?"

Sebastian didn't know what it was about this woman that drew him so powerfully. He was involved in grave matters that required his full attention, yet for the life of him, he couldn't take his gaze from her.

She wore her honey-brown hair swept up so that it cascaded in riotous waves from a silver clip of old Welsh design. Several strands of it had come free of the clip to dangle haphazardly around her face as if the strands had a life of their own.

How he longed to set free that hair and feel it sliding through his fingers and brushing against his naked chest.

He dropped his gaze down over her lush, full body and stifled his smile. Her dark blue shirt wasn't buttoned properly and her socks didn't match.

Still, she drove him crazy with desire.

She wasn't the kind of woman who normally drew his interest, and yet . . .

He was beguiled by her and her crystal blue gaze that glowed with warm curiosity and intelligence. He longed to sample her full, moist lips, to bury his face in the hollow of her throat where he could drink in her scent.

Gods, how he yearned for her. It was a need borne of such desperation that he wondered what kept him from taking her into his arms right now and satisfying his curiosity.

He'd never been the kind of man to deny himself carnal pleasures—especially not when the beast inside him was stirred. And this woman stirred that deadly part of him to a dangerous level.

Sebastian had only come into the museum to get the lay of it for tonight and to find out where they housed the tapestry. He hadn't been looking for a woman to pass the lonely night with until he could return home where he would be . . . well, lonely again.

However, he still had hours before he could leave. Hours that he would much rather spend gazing into her eyes than waiting in his hotel room.

"Would you care to join me for a drink?" he asked.

She looked startled by his question. But then he seemed to have that effect on her. She was nervous around him, a bit jumpy, and he longed to set her at ease.

"I don't go out with men I don't know."

"How can you get to know me unless you . . ."

"Really, Mr. Kat—"

"Sebastian."

She shook her head at him. "You are persistent, aren't you?"

She had no idea.

Suppressing the predator inside him, Sebastian put his hands in his pockets to keep from reaching out to her and scaring her off. "I'm afraid it's ingrained in me. When I see something I want, I go after it."

She arched a brow at that and gave him a suspicious look. "Why on earth would you want to talk to me?"

He was aghast at her question. "My lady, do you not own a mirror?"

"Yes, but it's not an enchanted one." She turned away from him and started away.

Moving with the incredible speed of his kind, Sebastian pulled her to a stop.

"Look, Channon," he said gently. "I fear I have bungled this. I just . . ." He stopped and tried to think of the best way to keep her with him for a while longer.

She looked to his hand, which still gripped her elbow. He reluctantly let go, even though every part of his soul screamed for him to hold her by his side, regardless of the consequences. She was a woman with her own mind. And the first law of his people ran through his head: Nothing a woman gives is worth having unless she gives it of her own free will.

It was the one law not even he would break.

"You what?" she asked softly.

Sebastian drew a deep breath as he fought down the animal part of himself that wanted her regardless of right or laws, the part of him that snarled with a need so fierce that it scared him.

He forced a charming smile to his lips. "You seem like a very nice person, and there are so few of you in this world that I would like to spend a few minutes with you. Maybe some of it might rub off."

Channon laughed in spite of herself.

"Ah," he teased, "so you *can* smile."

"I can smile."

"Will you join me?" he asked. "There's a restaurant on the corner. We can walk there, in plain sight of the world. I promise, I won't bite unless you ask me to."

Channon frowned lightly at him and his quirky humor. What was it about him that made him so irresistible? It was unnatural. "I don't know about this."

"Look, I promise I'm not psychotic. Eccentric and idiosyncratic, but not psychotic."

She still wasn't completely sure about that. "I'll bet the prisons are full of men who have told women that."

"I would *never* hurt a woman, least of all you."

There was such sincerity in his voice that she believed him. Even more convincing, she didn't feel any inner warnings, no little voice in her head telling her to run.

Instead, she was drawn to him and felt a most peculiar kind of serenity in his presence, almost as if she were supposed to be with him. "Down the street?"

"Yes." He offered her his arm. "C'mon. I promise I'll keep my fangs hidden and my mind control to myself."

Channon had never done anything like this in her life. She was a woman who had to know a guy for a long time before she'd even consider a date.

Yet she found herself pulling on her coat and placing her hand in the crook of his arm, where she felt a muscle so taut and well formed that it sent a jolt through her.

By the feel of that arm, she could tell his fashionable black suit and overcoat hid one incredible body.

"You seem so different," she said as he walked her out of the room. "Something about you is very Old World."

He opened the glass door that led to the museum's foyer. "*Old* being the operative word."

"And yet you're very modern."

"A Renaissance man trapped between cultures."

"Is that what you are?"

He cast a playful sideways look to her. "Honestly?"

"Yes."

"I'm a dragon slayer."

She laughed out loud.

He scoffed. "Again you don't believe me."

"Let's just say it's no wonder you said you wanted to steal the tapestry. I suppose there's not much call for slaying a mythological beast, especially in this day and age."

Those greenish-gold eyes teased her unmercifully. "You don't believe in dragons?"

"No, of course not."

He tsked at her. "You are so skeptical."

"I'm practical."

Sebastian ran his tongue over his teeth as a sly half-smile curved his lips. A practical woman who didn't believe in dragons yet studied dragon tapestries and wore a misbuttoned shirt. Surely there wasn't another soul like her in any time or place. And she had the strangest effect on his body.

He was already hard for her, and they were barely touching. Her grip on his arm was light and delicate, as if she was ready to flee him at any moment.

That was the last thing he wanted, and that surprised him most of all.

A reclusive person, he only interacted with others when his physical needs overrode his desire for solitude. Even then, those encounters were brief and limited. He took his lovers for one night, making sure they were as well sated as he, then he quickly returned to his solitary world.

He'd never dawdled with idle conversation. Never really cared to get to know more about a woman than her name and the way she liked to be touched.

But Channon was different. He liked the cadence of her voice and the way her eyes sparkled when she talked. Most of all, he liked the way her smile lit up her entire face when she looked at him.

And the sound of her laughter . . . He doubted if the angels in heaven could make a more precious melody.

Sebastian opened the door to the dark restaurant and held it for her while she entered. As she swept past him, he let his gaze travel down the back of her body. He hardened even more.

What he wouldn't give to have her warm and naked in his arms so that he could run his hands down her full curves, nibble the flesh of her neck, and hold her to him as he slowly slid himself deep inside her while she writhed to his touch.

Sebastian forced himself to look away from Channon and to speak to the hostess. He sent a mental command to the unknown woman to sit them in a secluded corner. He wanted privacy with Channon.

How he wished he'd met her sooner. He'd been in this cursed city for well over a week, waiting for the opportunity to go home, where if not the comfort of warmth, he at least had the comfort of familiarity. He'd spent his nights in this city alone, prowling the streets restlessly as he bided his time.

At dawn, he would have to leave. But until then, he intended to spend as much time with Channon as he could, letting her company ease the loneliness inside him, ease the pain in his heart that had burned him for most of his life.

Channon followed the hostess through the restaurant, but all the while she was aware of Sebastian behind her—aware of his hot, predatorial gaze on her body and the way he seemed to want to devour her.

But even more unbelievable was the fact that she wanted to devour *him*. No man had ever made her feel so much like a woman or made her want to spend hours exploring his body with her hands and mouth.

"You're nervous again," he said after they were seated in a dark corner in the back of the pub.

She glanced up from the menu to catch sight of those greenish-gold eyes that reminded her of some feral beast. "You are incredibly perceptive."

He inclined his head toward her. "I've been accused of worse."

"I'll bet you have," she teased back. Indeed, he had the presence of an outlaw. Dangerous, dark, seductive. "Are you really a thief?"

"Define the term *thief.*"

She laughed even though she wasn't quite sure if he was joking or serious.

"So tell me," he said as the waitress brought their drinks, "what do you do for a living, Shannon with a C?"

She thanked the waitress for her Coke, then looked to Sebastian to see how he would deal with her occupation. Most men were a bit intimidated by her job, though she'd never been able to figure out why. "I'm a history professor at the University of Virginia."

"Impressive," he said, his face genuinely interested. "What cultures and times do you specialize in?"

She was amazed he knew anything about her job. "Mostly preNorman Britain."

"Ah. Hwæt wē Gār-Dena in geār-dagum Þēod-cyninga Þrym gefrūnon, hū ðā æÞhelingas ellen fremedon."

Channon was floored by his Old English. He spoke it as if he'd been born to it. Imagine a man so handsome knowing a subject so dear to her heart.

She offered him the translation. "So. The Spear-Danes in days gone by and the kings who ruled them had courage and greatness. We have heard of those princes' heroic campaigns."

His inclined his head to her. "You know your *Beowulf* well."

"I've studied Old English extensively, which, given my job, makes sense. But you don't strike me as a historian."

"I'm not. Rather, I'm a sort of reenactor."

That explained the way he looked. Now his presence in the museum and knightly air of authority made sense to her.

"Is your study of the Middle Ages what had you in the museum today?" he asked.

She nodded. "I've studied the tapestry for years. I want to be the person who finally unravels the mystery behind it."

"What would you like to know?"

"Who made it and why? Where the story of it comes from. For that matter, I would love to know how the museum got it. They have no record of when they acquired it or from whom it was purchased."

His automatic answers surprised her. "They bought it in 1926 from an anonymous collector for fifty thousand dollars. As for the rest, it was made by a woman named Antiphone back in seventh-century Britain. It's the story of her grandfather and his brother and their eternal struggle between good and evil."

His gaze was so sincere that she could almost believe him. In a strange way, it made sense, since the tapestry had no ending.

But she knew better. "Antiphone, huh?"

He shook his head. "You just don't believe anything I tell you, do you?"

"Why, kind sir," she said impishly with a mock English accent. " 'Tis not that I don't believe you, but as a historian I must align myself with fact. Have you any proof of this Antiphone or transaction?"

"I do, but I somehow doubt you would appreciate my showing it to you."

"And why is that?"

"It would scare the life out of you."

Channon sat back at that, unsure of how to take it. She didn't really know what to make of the man sitting across from her. He kept her on edge all the while he lured her toward his danger. Lured her against all her reason.

They remained quiet as their food was placed on the table.

While they ate, Channon studied him. The candlelight in the pub danced in his eyes, making them glow like a cat's. His hands were strong and callused—the hands of a man who was used to hard work—yet he had the air of wealth and privilege, the air of a powerful man who made his own rules.

He was a total enigma, a walking dichotomy who made her feel both safe and threatened.

"Tell me, Channon," he said suddenly, "do you like teaching?"

"Some days. But it's the research I like best. I love digging through old manuscripts and trying to piece together the past."

He gave a short half laugh. "No offense, but that sounds incredibly boring."

"I imagine dragon-slaying is much more action-oriented."

"Yes, it is. Every moment is completely unpredictable."

She wiped her mouth as she watched him eat with perfect European table manners. He was definitely cultured, yet he seemed oddly barbaric. "So, how do you kill a dragon?"

"With a very sharp sword."

She shook her head at him. "Yes, but do you call him out? Do you go to him . . . ?"

"The easiest way is to sneak up on him."

"And pray he doesn't wake up?"

"Well, it makes it more challenging if he does."

Channon smiled. She was so drawn to that infectious wit of his. Especially since he didn't seem to notice the women around them who were ogling him while they ate. It was as if he could only see her.

As a rule, she stunk at this whole male-female thing. Her last boyfriend, a D.C. correspondent, had educated her well on every personal and physical flaw she possessed. The last thing she was looking for was another relationship in which she wasn't on equal terms with the man.

For her next love interest, she wanted someone just like her—a historian of average looks whose life revolved around research. Two comfortable peas in a pod.

She wasn't looking for some hot, mysterious stranger who made her blood burn with desire.

Channon, would you listen to yourself and what you're saying! You are insane not to want this man!

Perhaps. But things like this never happened to her.

"You know," she said to him, "I keep having this really weird feeling that you're going to take me someplace later and tie me up naked so that your friends can come laugh at me."

He arched a brow at her. "Does that happen to you often?"

"No, never, but this night has the makings for a *Twilight Zone* episode."

"I promise no Rod Serling voice-overs. You're safe with me."

And for some reason that made absolutely no sense whatsoever, she believed him.

Channon spent the next few hours having the dinner and conversation of her life. Sebastian was incredibly easy to talk to. Worse, he set her hormones on fire.

The longer they were together and the more laughs they shared, and the more incredible he seemed.

She glanced at her watch and gasped. "Did you know it's almost midnight?"

He checked his watch.

"I hate to cut this short," she said, placing her napkin on the table and sliding her chair back, "but I have to go or I'll never get a taxi out of here."

He placed his hand lightly on her arm to keep her at the table. "Why don't you let me drive you home?"

Channon started to protest, but something inside her refused. After the evening they had spent together, she felt oddly at ease with him. There was an aura about him that was so comforting, so open and welcoming.

He was like a long lost friend.

"Okay," she said, relaxing.

He paid for their food. Then he helped her up and into her coat and led her from the restaurant.

Channon didn't speak as they made their way toward his car down the street, but she felt his magnetic, masculine presence with every single cell of her body.

Though not a social butterfly by any account, she'd had plenty of dates in her life. She'd had a number of boyfriends and even a fiancé, but none of them had ever made her feel the way this stranger did.

Like he fit some missing part of her soul.

Girl, you are crazy.

She must be.

Channon paused as they neared his sporty gray Lexus. "Someone travels in style."

Winking devilishly at her, Sebastian opened the car door. "Well, I would turn into a dragon and fly you home, but something tells me you would protest."

"No doubt. I imagine the scales would also chafe my skin."

"True. Not to mention, I once learned the hard way that they really do call the military out on you. You know, fighter jets are hard to dodge when you have a forty-foot wingspan." He closed her door and walked to his side of the car.

She laughed yet again, but then she'd been doing that most of the night. Goodness, she *really* liked this man.

Sebastian got into the car and felt his body jerk the instant they were locked inside together. Her feminine scent permeated his head. She was so close to him now that he could almost taste her.

All night long he had listened to the dulcet sound of her smooth Southern drawl, watched her tongue and lips move as he imagined what they would feel like on his body, imagined her in his arms while he made love to her until she cried out from pleasure.

His attraction to her stunned him. Why did he have to feel this now, when he couldn't afford to stay in her time and explore more of her?

Cursed Fates. How they loved to tamper in mortal lives.

Pushing the thought out of his mind, he drove her to the hotel where she was staying.

"You don't live here?" he asked as he parked in the lot.

"Just here for the weekend to study the tapestry." She unbuckled her seat belt.

Sebastian got out and opened her door, then walked her to her room.

Channon hesitated at the door as she looked up at him and the searing heat in his captivating eyes. The man was so hot and sexy in the most dangerous of ways.

She wondered if she would ever see him again. He hadn't asked for her number. Not even her email.

Damn.

"Thank you," she said. "I had a really good time tonight."

"I did, too. Thanks for joining me."

Kiss me. The words rushed across her mind unexpectedly. She really wanted to know what this man felt like against her.

To her amazement, she found out as he pulled her into his arms and covered her lips with his.

Sebastian growled at the feel of her as he fisted his hands against her back. He clutched her to him as every fiber of his body burned and ached to possess her. Her tongue swept against his, teasing him, tormenting him.

She brushed her hand against the nape of his neck, sending chills all over his body, making him so hard for her that he throbbed painfully. He closed his eyes while he let all of his senses experience her. Her mouth tasted of honey, and her hands were soft and warm against his skin. She smelled of woman and flowers, and he thrilled at the sound of her ragged breathing as she answered his passion with her own.

Take her. The animal inside him stirred with a fierce snarl. It snapped and clawed at the human part of him, demanding he cede his humanity to it. It wanted her.

He was almost powerless against the onslaught, and his hands trembled from the force of holding himself back. He growled from the effort of it.

Channon moaned at the fierce feel of his powerful arms locked around her. She was pressed so tight against his chest that she could feel his heart pounding against her breasts.

His intensity surrounded her, filled her, made her burn with volcanic need. All she could think of was stripping his clothes off him and seeing if his body really was as spectacular as it felt.

He pressed her back against her door, pinning her to it as he deepened his kiss. His warm, masculine scent filled her senses, overwhelming her.

He kissed his way from her lips and down across her cheek, then he buried his lips against her neck. "Let me make love to you, Channon," he breathed in her ear. "I want to feel your warm, soft body against mine. Feel your breath on my naked skin."

She should be offended by his suggestion. They barely knew each other. Yet no matter how hard she tried to talk herself out of this, she couldn't.

Deep inside, she wanted the same thing.

Against all reason—all sanity—she ached for him.

Never in her life had she done anything like this. Not once. Yet she found herself opening the door to her room and letting him in.

Sebastian breathed deeply in relief as he struggled for control. He'd never come so close to using his powers on a woman. It was forbidden for his kind to interfere with human freewill unless it was in defense of their lives or someone else's. He'd bent that rule a time or two to serve his purposes.

Tonight, had she refused him, he held no doubt he would have broken it.

But she hadn't refused him. Thank the gods for small favors.

He watched her as she set her key card on the dresser. She hesitated and he felt her nervousness.

"I won't hurt you, Channon."

She offered him a tentative smile. "I know."

He cupped her face in his hands and stared into those celestial blue eyes. "You are so beautiful."

Channon held her breath as he pulled her to him and recaptured her lips. None of this night made sense to her. None of her feelings. She clung to Sebastian as she sought for an explanation why she had let him into her room.

Why she was going to make love to him. A stranger. A man she knew nothing about. A man she would like as not never see again.

Yet none of that mattered. All that mattered was this moment in time—holding him close to her and keeping him here in her room for as long as she could.

She felt his hands free her hair to cascade down her back. He slid her coat from her shoulders, and she let it fall to the floor. Running his hands up her arms, he pulled back to stare down at her with hungry eyes. No man had ever given her such a look. One of fierce longing, of total possession.

Scared and excited, she helped him from his overcoat. His eyes dark with unsated passion, he removed his jacket and tossed it aside without care that it would be wrinkled later. So much for his impeccable suit. It thrilled her that she meant more to him than that.

He loosened his tie and pulled it over his head.

His eyes softened as she moved to unbutton his shirt. He caught her right hand in his and nibbled her fingertips, sending ribbons of pleasure through her, then he led her hand to his buttons and watched her intently.

Hot and aching for him, Channon worked the buttons through the buttonholes of his shirt. She trailed her gaze after her hands, watching as she bared his skin inch by slow, studied inch. Oh, good heaven, the man had a body that had been ripped from her dreams. His muscles were tight and perfect and covered by the most luscious tawny skin she'd ever seen. Dark hairs dusted his skin, making him seem even more like a predator, even more dangerous and manly.

Channon paused at the hard abs that held several scars. She traced her hand over them, feeling his sharp intake of breath as her fingers brushed the raised, lighter skin. "What happened?"

"Dragons have sharp talons," he whispered. "Sometimes I don't get out of the way quickly enough."

She placed her hand over one really nasty-looking scar by his hipbone. "Maybe you should fight smaller dragons."

"That wouldn't be very sporting of me."

She swallowed as he removed his shirt and she saw his unadorned chest for the first time. He was scrumptious. She ran her palm over his taut, hard pecs, delighting in the way they felt under her hands. She ran her fingers up his chest and across his lean, hard shoulder, which was tattooed with a dragon. "You do like dragons, don't you?"

He laughed. "Yes, I do."

Sebastian was doing his best to be patient, to let her get used to him. But it was hard when all he really wanted to do was lay her down on the bed and relieve the fierce ache in his loins.

He nibbled at her neck as he unfastened the buttons on her jumper and let it fall to the floor. She stood before him wearing nothing but her shoes and her misbuttoned shirt. It was the sexiest thing he'd ever seen in his four hundred years of living. "Do you always button your shirts like this?"

She looked down and gasped. "Oh, good grief. I was in a hurry this morning and—"

He stopped her words with a kiss. "Don't apologize," he whispered against her lips. "I like it."

"You're a very strange man."

"And you are a goddess."

Channon shook her head at him as he picked her up in his arms and moved with her toward the bed. She placed her hands over his muscles, which were taut from his strain. The feel of them made her mouth water. He laid her gently on the mattress, then ran his hands down her legs to her feet so he could remove her shoes and socks and toss them over his shoulder.

Her heart pounding, Channon watched as he nibbled his way over her hip to her stomach. He moved his hands to her shirt and slowly unbuttoned it, kissing and licking every piece of her skin that he bared.

She moaned at the sight and feel of his mouth on her, at the way he seemed to savor her body. Spikes of pleasure pierced her stomach as her body throbbed and ached for him to fill her.

She wanted him inside her so much that she feared she might burst into flames from the fire tearing through her body.

Sebastian felt her wetness on his skin as he slid himself against her. His body screamed for hers, but he wasn't through with her yet. He wanted to savor her, to commit every inch of her lush body to his memory.

What he felt for her amazed him. It was unlike anything he'd ever experienced. On some strange level she gave him peace, sanctuary. She filled the loneliness in his battered heart.

He buried his face in her neck while her hardened nipples teased the flesh of his chest and her hands roamed over his back. "You feel so good under me," he whispered as he soaked her essence into him.

Channon took a deep, ragged breath. His words delighted her.

He nuzzled her neck, his whiskers softly teasing her flesh while his hand skimmed over her body to touch the burning ache between her legs. She hissed at the pleasure of his fingers toying with her and arched her back against him as he slowly dragged his mouth from her neck to her breast. His tongue swept against the hardened tip, making her tingle and throb.

She bit her lip as a wave of fear went through her. "I want you to know that I don't normally do this sort of thing."

He lifted himself up on his arms to look down at her. He pressed his hips between her legs so that she could feel the large bulge of him while his expensive wool pants slightly chafed her inner thighs. The hot feel of him there was enough to drive her wild with need.

"If I thought you did, my lady, I wouldn't be here with you now." His gaze intensified, holding her enthralled. "I see you, Channon. You and the barriers you have around you that keep everyone at a distance."

"And yet you're here."

"I'm here because I know the sadness inside you. I know what it feels like to wake in the morning, lost and lonely and aching for someone to be there with me."

Her heart clenched as he spoke the very things that really were a part of her. "Why are *you* alone? I can't imagine a man so handsome without a line of willing women fighting behind him."

"Looks aren't all there is in this world, my lady. They are certainly no protection against being alone. Hearts never see through the eyes."

Channon swallowed at his words. Did he mean them? Or was this all some lie he was telling her to make her feel better about what she was doing with him? She didn't know.

But she wanted to believe him. She wanted to comfort the torment she saw in his hungry eyes.

He pulled away from her and removed his shoes and pants. Channon trembled as she finally saw him completely naked. Like a dangerous, dark beast moving sinuously in the moonlight, he was incredible. Absolutely stunning.

Every inch of him was muscled and toned and covered by the most scrumptious tanned skin she'd ever beheld. The only flaws on his perfect body were the scars marking his back, hips, and legs. They really did look like claw and bite marks from some ferocious beast.

When he rejoined her on the bed, she pulled the tie from his hair, letting it fall forward to surround his sinfully handsome face.

"You look like some barbaric chieftain," she said, running her hand through the silkiness of his unbound hair. She traced the intricate lines of the tattoo on his face.

"Mmm," he breathed, taking her breast in his mouth.

Channon held his head to her as his tongue teased her. Ripples of pleasure tore through her.

She ran her hands down his muscled ribs, then along his arms and shoulders as she drifted through a strange hazy fog of pleasure. Something strange was happening to her. With every breath he expelled, it was like his touch intensified. Multiplied. Instead of one tongue stroking her, she swore she could feel a hundred of them. It was as if her skin was alive and being massaged all over at once.

Sebastian hissed as his powers ran through him. Sex always heightened the senses of his breed. The intensity of physical pleasure was highly sought by his people for the elevation it gave them and their magic. The beauty of it was that the surge of power usually lasted a full day, and in the case of truly great sex, two days.

Channon was definitely a two-day high.

He looked into her eyes to see her gaze unfocused and wild. His powers were affecting her, too. The physical stimulation to a human was even greater than it was to his breed.

He knew the moment she lost herself to the ecstasy of his sorcerer's touch. Her barriers and inhibitions gone, she threw her head back and cried out as an orgasm tore through her. "That's it," he whispered in her ear. "Don't fight it."

She didn't. Instead, she turned toward him and grabbed feverishly at his body. Sebastian groaned as he obliged her eagerness.

She sought out every inch of his flesh with her hands and mouth. He rolled over and pulled her on top of him, where she straddled his waist, letting him feel her wetness on the hollow of his stomach. He knew she was past the ability to speak now and a part of him regretted that. She was all need. All hot, demanding sex.

Her eyes wild and hungry, she took his hands in hers and led them to her breasts as she slid herself against his swollen shaft. She leaned forward to drag her tongue along the edge of his jaw as she nibbled her way to his lips.

She kissed him passionately, then pulled back. "What have you done to me?" she asked hoarsely, her words surprising him.

"It's not exactly me," he said honestly. "It's something I can't help."

She moaned and writhed against him, making his body burn even more. "I need you inside me, Sebastian. Please."

He wasted no time obliging her. Rolling her over, he curled his body around hers as they lay with her back to his front. He draped her leg over his waist.

He tucked her head beneath his chin and held her close as he drove himself deep inside her sleek wetness. He growled at the warm, wet feel of her while she leaned her head back into his shoulder and cried out.

Channon had never felt anything like this. No man had

ever made love to her in such a manner. Her right hip was braced against his inner thigh while he used his left knee to hold her left leg up so that he had access to her body from behind her. She didn't know how he managed it, but his strokes were deep and even, and they tore through her with the most intense pleasure she had ever known. He was so hard inside her, so thick and warm.

And she wanted more of his touch. More of his power.

He slid his hand down over her stomach, then lower until he touched her between her legs. She hissed and writhed as pleasure tore through her while his fingers rubbed her in time to his strokes. And still it felt as if a thousand hands caressed her, as if she were being bathed all over by his touch, his scent.

Out of her mind with ecstasy, she met him lush stroke for lush stroke. Her body felt as if it held a life of its own, as if the pleasure of her was its own entity. She needed even more of him.

Sebastian was awed by her response to him. No human woman had ever been like this. If he didn't know better, he'd swear she was part Drakos. She dug her nails into the flesh of the arms he had wrapped around her, and when she came again she screamed out so loudly, he had to quickly put a dampening spell around them to keep others from hearing her.

His powers surging, he smiled wickedly at that. He loved satisfying his partner, and with Channon he took even more delight than normal.

She rolled slightly in his arms, capturing his lips in a frenzied kiss.

Sebastian cupped her face as he quickened his strokes and buried himself even deeper in her body. She felt so incredibly good to him. So warm and welcoming. So perfect.

He held her close against him as his heart pounded and his groin tightened even more. The feel of her, the taste of her, cascaded through his senses, making him reel, making him ache, yet at the same time soothing him.

The beast in him roared and snapped in satisfaction while the man buried himself deep in her and shook from the force of his orgasm. With the two parts of him sated and united, it was the most incredible moment of his entire life.

Channon groaned as she felt his release inside her. Still wrapped around her, he pulled her even closer to his chest. She heard his ragged breathing and felt his heart pounding against her shoulder blade. The manly scent of him filled her head and her heart, making her want to stay cocooned by his body forever.

Slowly, the throbbing pleasure faded from her and left her weak and drained from the intensity of their lovemaking.

When he withdrew from her, she felt a tremendous sense of loss.

"What did you do to me?" she asked, turning onto her back to look at him.

He kissed his way across her collarbone to her lips. "I did nothing, *ma petite*. It was all you."

"Trust me, I've never done that before."

He laughed softly in her ear.

She smiled at him and dropped her gaze to the small gold medallion he wore around his neck. Odd, she hadn't noticed it before.

She traced the chain with her fingers, then took it into her hand. It was obviously quite old. Ancient Greek if she didn't miss her guess. The gold held a relief of a dragon coiled around a shield. "This is beautiful," she breathed.

Sebastian looked down at her hand and covered her fingers with his. "It belonged to my mother," he said, wondering why he spoke of it. It was something he'd never shared with anyone else. "I don't really remember her, but my brother said she told him to give it to me so that I would know how much she loved me."

"She died?"

He nodded. "I was barely six when . . ." His voice trailed off as his memories of that night scorched him. Inside his head he could still hear the screams of the dying and smell the fires. He remembered the terror and the arms of his brother, Theren, pulling him to safety.

He'd always lived with the horrors of that night close to his heart. Tonight, with Channon, it didn't seem to hurt quite so much.

She ran her hand over the markings on his face. "I'm sorry," she whispered, and inside his heart, he could feel her sincerity. "I was nine when my mother died of cancer. And there's always this little piece of me that wishes I could hear the sound of her voice just one more time."

"You're without family?"

She nodded. "I grew up with my aunt, who died two years ago."

He felt her ache inside his own heart and it surprised him. He hated that she was alone in the world. Like him. It was a hard way to be.

Tightening his arms, he let his body comfort her.

Channon closed her eyes as he ran his tongue around and into her ear, sending chills over her. She leaned into his arms and pulled him close for another scorching kiss. A tiny part of her wanted to beg him not to leave her in the morning. But she refused to embarrass herself.

She'd known going into this that tonight would be all they would ever have. Yet the thought of not seeing him again hurt her more than she could fathom. She literally felt that losing him would be like losing a vital part of herself.

Sebastian knew he should leave now, but something inside him rebelled.

It wasn't much longer until dawn. He still had to retrieve the tapestry and return home.

But right now, all he wanted was to spend a little more time holding this woman, keeping her in the warm shelter of his arms.

"Sleep, Channon," he whispered as he sent a small sleeping spell to her. If she were awake and looking at him, he would never be able to let her go.

Immediately, she went limp in his arms.

Sebastian ran his fingers over the delicate curve of her cheek as he watched her. She was so beautiful by his side.

He clenched his hand against her silken curls and took a deep breath in her hair. Her floral scent reminded him of warm summer days of shared laughter and friendship. Her bare hips were nestled perfectly against his groin, her lower back against his stomach. Her smooth legs were entwined with his masculine ones. Gods, how he ached to keep her here like this.

He felt himself stirring again. He felt the need within him to take her one more time before he upheld his obligation.

You must go.

As much as he hated to, he knew he had no choice.

Sighing in regret, he withdrew from the warmth of her and crept from the bed, still amazed by the night they had shared. He would never forget her. And for the first time in his life, he actually considered coming back here for a while.

But that was impossible.

His kind didn't do well in the modern world, where they were easily hunted and found. He needed wide-open spaces and a simpler world where he could have the freedom and solitude he needed.

Clenching his teeth against the pain of necessity, he dressed silently in the dark.

Sebastian stepped away from the bed, then paused.

He couldn't leave like this, as if the night had meant nothing to him.

Pulling his mother's medallion from his neck, he placed it around Channon's and kissed her parted lips.

"Sleep, little one," he whispered. "May the Fates be kind to you. Always."

Then, he shimmered from her room and out into the dark night. Alone. He was always alone.

He'd long ago accepted that fact. It was what had to be.

But tonight he felt that loneliness more profoundly than he had ever felt it before.

As he rounded the hotel's building and headed toward his car, he collided with a middle-aged woman who was walking, huddled from the cold, in a worn jacket. She wore the faded uniform of a waitress and the old shoes of a woman who had no choice but to be practical.

"Hey," he said as she started past him. "Do you have a car?"

She shook her head no.

"You do now." He handed her the keys to his Lexus and pointed it out to her. "You'll find the registration in the glove box. Just fill it out and it's yours."

She blinked at him. "Yeah, right."

Sebastian offered her a genuine smile. He'd only bought the car to use while he'd been trapped in this time period. Where he was going, there was no need for it.

"I'm serious," he said, nudging her toward it. "No strings attached. I took a vow of poverty about fifteen minutes ago, and it's all yours."

She laughed incredulously. "I have no idea who you are, but thank you."

Sebastian inclined his head and waited until the woman had driven off.

Cautiously, he stepped into the alley and looked around to make sure there were no witnesses. He called forth the powers of Night to shield him from anyone who might happen by, then he shifted into his alternate form. The power of the Drakos rushed through him like fire as the ions in the air around him were charged with electrical energy—electrical energy that allowed him to shed one form and shift into another.

In his case, his alternate form was that of a dragon.

Spreading his bloodred wings out to their full forty-foot span, he launched himself from his hind legs and flew into the sky, careful to stay below radar level this time.

Sebastian had one last thing to do before he could return to his time. Yet even as he headed back to the museum, he couldn't shake the image of Channon from his mind.

He could still see her asleep in the bed, her hair spread out around her shoulders. He could still feel the texture of the honey-laced strands in his palm.

His dragon form burned with need, and he yearned to return to her.

Not that he could. One-night stands with humans were all he dared. The risk of exposure was too great.

Sebastian crossed town in a matter of minutes and landed on the roof of the museum. He summoned the electrical field that allowed the molecules of his body to transform from animal to human and flashed back into his man form.

With a flick of his hand, he dressed himself all in black, then shimmered from the roof into the room that held the tapestry.

"There you are," he said as he saw Antiphone's work again. Sadness, guilt, and grief tore through him as he recalled his baby sister's gentle face.

After he'd sold this tapestry, he had never wanted to see it again.

But now he had to have it. It was the only way to save his brother's life. Not that he should care. Damos had never given a damn about him.

After all the things Damos had done to break him, Sebastian still couldn't turn his back on his brother and let the man die. Not when he could help it.

"I'm a bloody fool," he said disgustedly.

He willed the tapestry from the museum case into his hand. Then he folded and tucked it carefully into a black leather bag to protect it.

As he began to shimmer from the room back to the roof, an odd burning started in the palm of his left hand.

"What the . . . ?"

Hissing from the pain, he dropped the case and pulled off his glove. Sebastian blew cool air across his hot skin and frowned as a round geometric design appeared in his palm.

"No," he breathed in disbelief as he stared at it.

This wasn't possible, yet there was no denying what he saw and felt. Worse, there was a presence inside him, a tickling in the depth of his heart that made him curse even louder.

Against his will, he was mated.

Two

This was a nightmare. The absolute worst *kind of night-*mare.

It was wrong. It had to be.

Sebastian left the museum immediately, all the while debating his next step. On the building's roof, he paused. He needed to take the tapestry back to Britain of a thousand years earlier. He was sworn to it. He'd destroyed Antiphone's future, and now the fate of his brother was in his hands.

But the mark . . .

He couldn't leave his mate here while he went home. Nor could he stay in this time period where the danger of being inadvertently struck by an electrical charge was so strong—that was his one Achilles' heel.

Because he relied on electrical impulses to change forms, any kind of outside electrical jolt could involuntarily transform him. It was why his kind avoided any time period after Benjamin Franklin, the so-called Satan of his people.

But Arcadian law demanded he protect his mate.

At any cost.

Centuries of war had left the Drakos branch of the Arcadians virtually extinct. And since Sebastian hunted down and executed the evil animal Drakos, their kind would make it a point to track and kill his mate should they ever learn of Channon's existence.

She would be dead and it would be all his fault.

Should she die, he would never mate again.

"Mate, my bloody hell," he muttered. He looked up at the clear, full moon above. "Damn you, Fates. What were you thinking?"

To mate a human to an Arcadian was cruel. It happened only rarely, so rarely that he'd never even considered the possibility of it. So why did it have to happen now?

Leave her.

He should. Yet if he did, he would leave behind his only chance for a family. Unlike a human male, he was only given one shot at this. If he failed to claim Channon, he would spend the rest of his exceptionally long life alone.

Completely alone.

No other woman would ever again appeal to him.

He would be doomed to celibacy.

Oh bloody, damned hell with that.

There was no choice. At the end of three weeks, the mark on her human hand would fade and she would forget he'd ever existed. The mark on his Arcadian hand was eternal, and he would mourn her for the rest of his life. Even if he went back for her later, it would be too late. After the mark faded, his chance was over.

It was now or never.

Not to mention the small fact that during the three weeks she was marked by his sign, Channon would be a magnet to the Katagaria Draki who wanted him dead.

For centuries, he and the animal Katagaria had played a deadly game of cat and mouse. The Katagaria routinely sent out mental feelers for him, just as he did for them. Their psychic sonar would easily pick up his mark on Channon's body, allowing them to hone in on her.

And if one of them were to find his mate alone without a protector . . .

He flinched at the image in his mind.

No, he had to protect her. That was all there was to it.

Closing his eyes, Sebastian transformed himself into the dragon and went back to Channon's hotel, where he shifted forms again and entered her room as a man.

He was about to break nine kinds of laws.

He laughed bitterly. So what else was new? And why should he care? His people had banished him long ago. He was dead to them. Why should he abide by their laws?

He didn't care about them.

He cared for nothing. For no one.

Yet as he stared at Channon lying asleep in the moonlight, something peculiar happened to him. A feeling of possessive need tore through him. She was his mate. His only salvation.

For whatever twisted reason, the Fates had joined them. To leave Channon here unprotected would be wrong. She had no idea the kind of enemies who would do anything to have him, enemies who wouldn't hesitate to hurt her because she was his.

Sebastian lay down by her side and gathered her into his arms. She murmured in her sleep, then snuggled into him. His heart pounded at the sensation of her breath against his neck.

He looked down and saw her right palm, which bore the same mark as his left hand, laying upright by her cheek. He'd waited an eternity for her.

After all these centuries of empty loneliness, dare he even dream of having a home again? A family?

Then again, dare he not?

"Channon?" he whispered softly, trying to wake her. "I need to ask you something."

"Hmm?" she murmured in her sleep.

"I can't remove you from your time period unless you agree to it. I need you to come with me. Will you?"

She blinked open her eyes and looked up at him with a sleepy frown. "Where are you taking me?"

"I want to take you home with me."

She smiled up at him like an angel, then sighed. "Sure."

Sebastian tightened his arms around her as she fell back to sleep. She'd said yes. Joy ripped through him. Maybe he had done his penance after all.

Maybe, for once, he could have his one moment of respite from the past.

Holding her close, Sebastian stared out the window and waited for the first rays of dawn so that he could pulse them out of her world and into one beyond her wildest imagination.

Channon felt a strange tugging in her stomach that settled into a terrible queasiness. What on earth?

She opened her eyes to see Sebastian staring down at her. He wore an intriguing mask of black and red feathers that made the gold of his eyes stand out even more prominently. It reminded her of a *Phantom of the Opera* mask as it only covered his forehead and the left side of his face where his tattoo was.

She'd never considered masks sexy before, but on him, mmm, baby.

Even more inviting than that, he wore black leather armor over a chain mail shirt—black leather armor covered in silver rings and studs that was laced down the front. The laces had come untied, leaving an enticing gap where she could see his tanned skin peeping through.

Ummm, hmmm.

Smiling, she started to speak until she realized she was

on the back of a horse. A really, really *big* horse.

Even more peculiar, she was dressed in a dark green gown with wide sleeves that flowed around her like some fairy-tale princess garment.

"Okay," she breathed, running her hand along the intricate gold embroidery on her sleeve. "It's a dream. I can cope with a dream where I'm Sleeping Beauty or something."

"It's not a dream," he said quietly.

Channon laughed nervously as she sat up in his lap and glanced around. The sun was high above as if it were well into the afternoon, and they were traveling on an old dirt road that ran perpendicular to a thick, prehistoric-looking forest.

Something was wrong. She could feel it in her bones, and she could tell by the stiffness of his body and his guarded look. He was hiding something. "Where are we?"

"The where of it," he said slowly, refusing to meet her gaze, "isn't nearly as interesting as the *when* part."

"Excuse me?"

She watched the emotions flicker in his eyes, but the most peculiar one was a fleeting look of panic, as if he were nervous about answering her question. "Do you remember last night when I asked if I could take you home with me and you said sure?"

Channon frowned. "Vaguely, yes."

"Well, honey, I'm home."

An ache started in her head. What was he talking about? "Home? Where?"

He cleared his throat and still refused to meet her gaze. The man was definitely hedging. But why?

"You said you like research, right?" he asked.

Her stomach knotted even more. "Yes."

"Consider this a unique research venture then."

"Meaning what?"

His jaw flexed. "Haven't you ever wished you could

go back to Saxon England and find out what it was really like before the Normans invaded?"

"Of course."

"Well, your wish is granted." He looked at her and flashed an insincere smile.

Okay, the guy was not Robin Williams, and unless she was missing something really important from last night, she didn't conjure him from a bottle. If he wasn't a genie . . .

She laughed nervously. "What are you saying?"

"We're in England. Or rather we're in what will one day soon become England. Right now, this kingdom is called Lindsey."

Channon went completely still. She knew all about the medieval Saxon kingdom, and this . . . this was not possible. No, there was no way she could be here. "You're joking with me again, aren't you?"

He shook his head.

Channon rubbed her forehead as she tried to make sense of all this. "Okay, you have slipped me a mickey. Great. When I sober up from this you do realize I will call the cops."

"Well, it'll be about nine hundred years before there are cops to call, about a hundred more years after that before you have a phone. But I'm willing to wait if you are."

Channon clenched her eyes shut as she tried to think past the throbbing ache in her skull. "So you're telling me that I'm not dreaming and I'm not drugged."

"Correct on both accounts."

"But I'm in Saxon England?"

He nodded.

"And you're a dragon slayer?"

"Ah, so you remember that part."

"Yes," she said reasonably, but with every word she spoke after that, her voice crescendoed into mild hysteria.

"What I don't remember is how the hell I got *here!*" she shouted, sending several birds into flight.

Sebastian winced.

She glared at him. "You told me there wouldn't be any Rod Serling voice-overs, yet here I am in the middle of a *Twilight Zone* episode. Oh, and let me guess the title of it, *Night of the Terminally Stupid!*"

"It's not as bad as all that," Sebastian said, trying to decide the best way to explain this to her. He didn't blame her for being angry. In fact, she was taking all this a lot better than he had dared hope. "I know this is hard for you."

"Hard for me? I don't even know where to begin. I did something I've never done in my life and then I wake up and you tell me you have supposedly time-warped me into the past, and I'm not sure if I'm insane or delusional or what. Why am I here?"

"I . . ." Sebastian wasn't sure what to answer. The truth was pretty much out of the question. *Channon, I practically kidnapped you because you are my mate and I don't want to be alone for the next three to four hundred years of my life.*

No, definitely not something a man told a woman on their first date. He would have to woo her. Quickly. And win her over to wanting to stay here with him.

Preferably before a dragon ate one of them.

"Look, why don't you just think of this as a great adventure. Instead of reading about the history you teach, you can live it for a couple weeks."

"What are you? Disney World?" she asked. "And I can't stay here for a couple weeks. I have a life in the twenty-first century. I will be fired from my job. I will lose my car and my apartment. Good grief, who will pick up my laundry?"

"If you stayed here with me, it wouldn't be a problem. You'd never have to worry about any of that again."

Channon was aghast at him. *Oh, God, please let this*

be some bizarre nightmare. She had to wake up. This could not possibly be real.

"No," she said to him, "you're right. I wouldn't have to worry about *any* of that in Saxon England. I'd only have to worry about the lack of hygiene, lack of plumbing, Viking invasions, being burned at the stake, lack of modern conveniences, and nasty diseases with no antibiotics. Good grief, I can't even get a Midol. Not to mention, I'll never find out what happens next week on *Buffy!*"

Sebastian let out an elongated, patient breath and gave her an apologetic look that somehow succeeded in quelling a good deal of her anger.

"Look," he said quietly, "I'll make a deal with you. Spend a few weeks with me here, and if you really can't stand it, I'll take you home as close to the departure time as I can manage. Okay?"

Channon still had a hard time grasping all this. "Do you swear you're not playing some weird mind game with me? I really am *here*, in Saxon England?"

"I swear it on my mother's soul. You are in Saxon England, and I can take you back home. And no, I'm not playing mind games with you."

Channon accepted that, even though she couldn't imagine why. It was just a feeling she had that he would never swear on his mother's soul unless he meant it.

"Can you really take me back to the precise moment I left?"

"Probably not the precise moment, but I can try."

"What do you mean, *try?*"

He flashed his dimples, then turned serious. "Time-walking isn't an exact science. You can only move through the time fields when the dawn meets the night, and only under the power of a full moon. The problem is on the arrival end. You can try to get someplace specific, but you have only about a ninety-five percent chance of success. I might get you back that day, but it could also be a week or two after."

"And that's the best you can do?"

"Hey, just be grateful I'm old. When an Arcadian first starts time-walking, we only have about a three percent chance of success. I once ended up on Pluto."

She laughed in spite of herself. "Are you serious?"

He nodded. "They're not kidding about it being the coldest planet."

Channon took a deep breath as she digested everything he'd told her. Was any of this real? She didn't know, any more than she knew whether or not he was being honest about returning her. He was still very guarded. "Okay, so I'm stuck here until the next full moon?"

"Yes."

Oh, good grief, no. Had she been the kind of woman to whine, she'd probably be whining. But Channon was always practical. "All right. I can handle this," she said, more for her benefit than his. "I'll just pretend I'm a Saxon chick and you . . ." Her voice trailed off as she recalled what he'd said about time-traveling. "Just how old are you?"

"My people don't age quite the same way humans do. Since we can time-walk, we have a much slower biological clock."

Oh, she really didn't like the way he said *humans,* and if he turned fangy on her, she was going to stake him right through the heart. But she would get back to that in a minute. First, she wanted to understand the age thing. "So you age like dog years?"

Sebastian laughed. "Something like that. By human age, I would be four hundred sixty-three years old."

Channon sat flabbergasted as she looked over his lean, hard body. He appeared to be in his early thirties, not his late four hundreds. "You're not joking with me at all, are you?"

"Not even a little. Everything I have told you since the moment I met you has been the honest truth."

"Oh, God," she said, breathing in slowly and carefully

to calm the panic that was again trying to surface. She knew it was real, yet she had a hard time believing it. It boggled her mind that people could walk through time and that she could really be in the Dark Ages.

Surely, it couldn't be this easy.

"I know there has to be more of a downside to all this. And I'm pretty sure here's where I find out you're some kind of vampire or something."

"No," he said quickly. "I'm not a vampire. I don't suck blood, and I don't do anything weird to sustain my life. I was born from my mother, just as you were. I feel the same emotions. I bleed red blood. And just like you, I will die at some unknown date in the future. I just come equipped with a few extra powers."

"I see. I'm a Toyota. You're a Lambourghini, and you can have really awesome sex."

He chuckled. "That's a good summation."

Summation, hell. This was unbelievable. Inconceivable. How had she gotten mixed up with something like this?

But as she looked up at him, she knew. He was compelling. That deadly air and animal magnetism—how could she have even hoped to resist him?

And she wondered if there were more men out there like him. Men of power and magic. Men who were so incredibly sexy that to look at them was to burn for them. "Are there more of you?"

"Yes."

She smiled evilly at the thought. "A *lot* more?"

He frowned before he answered. "There used to be a lot more of us, but times change."

Channon saw the sadness in his eyes, the pain that he kept inside. It made her hurt for him.

He looked down at her. "That tapestry you love so much is the story of our beginning."

"The birth of the dragon and the man?"

He nodded. "About five thousand years before you were born, my grandfather, Lycaon, fell in love with a woman he thought was a human. She wasn't. She was born to a race that had been cursed by the Greek gods. She never told him who and what she really was, and in time she bore him two sons."

Channon remembered seeing that birth scene embroidered on the upper left edge of the tapestry.

"On her twenty-seventh birthday," he continued, "she died horribly just as all the members of her race die. And when my grandfather saw it, he knew his children were destined for the same fate. Angry and grief-stricken, he sought unnatural means to keep his children alive."

Sebastian was tense as he spoke. "Crazed from his grief and fear, he started capturing as many of my grandmother's people as he could and began experimenting with them—combining their life forces with those of animals. He wanted to make a hybrid creature that wasn't cursed."

"It worked?" she asked.

"Better than he had hoped. Not only did his sorcery give them the animal's strength and powers, it gave them a life span ten times longer than that of a human."

She arched a brow at that. "So you're telling me that you're a werewolf who lives seven or eight hundred years?"

"Yes on the age, but I'm not a Lykos. I'm a Drakos."

"You say that as if I have a clue about what you mean."

"Lycaon used his magic to 'half' his children. Instead of two sons, he made four."

"What are you saying?" she asked. "He sliced them down the middle?"

"Yes and no. There was a byproduct of the magic I don't think my grandfather was prepared for. When he combined a human and an animal, he expected his magic would create only one being. Instead, it made two of them. One person who held the heart of a human, and a separate creature whose heart was that of the animal.

"Those who have human hearts are called Arcadians. We are able to suppress the animal side of our nature. To control it. Because we have human hearts, we have compassion and higher reasoning."

"And the ones with animal hearts?"

"They are called Katagaria, meaning miscreant or rogue. Because of their animal hearts, they lack human compassion and are ruled by their baser instincts. Like their human brethren, they hold the same psychic abilities and shape-shifting, time-bending powers, but not the self-control."

That didn't sound good to her. "And the other people who were experimented on? Were there two of them, too?"

"Yes. And we formed the basis of two societies: the Arcadians and the Katagaria. As with nature, like went with like, and we created groups or patrias based on our animals. Wolf lives with wolf, hawk with hawk, dragon with dragon. We use Greek terms to differentiate between them. Therefore dragon is drakos, wolf is lykos, etcetera."

That made sense to her. "And all the while the Arcadians stayed with the Arcadians and Katagaria with Katagaria?"

"For the most part, yes."

"But I take it from the sound of your voice that no one lived happily-ever-after."

"No. The Fates were furious that Lycaon dared thwart them. To punish him, they ordered him to kill the creature-based children. He refused. So, the gods cursed us all."

"Cursed you how?"

A tic started in his jaw, and she saw the deep-seated agony in his eyes. "For one thing, we don't hit puberty until our mid-twenties. Because it is delayed, when it hits, it hits us hard. Many of us are driven to madness, and if we don't find a way to control and channel our powers we can become Slayers."

"I take it you don't mean the good vampire slayer kind of slayer that kills evil things."

"No. These are creatures that are bent on absolute destruction. They kill without remorse and with total barbarism."

"How awful," she breathed.

He agreed. "Until puberty, our children are either human or animal, depending on the parents' base-forms."

"Base-forms? What are those?"

"Arcadians are human so their base-forms are human. The Katagaria have a base-form of whatever animal part they are related to. An Ursulan would be a bear, a Gerakian would be a hawk."

"A Drakos would be a dragon."

He nodded. "A child has no powers at all, but with the onset of puberty, all the powers come in. We try to contain those who are going through it and teach them how to harness their powers. Most of the time we succeed as Arcadians, but with the Katagaria this isn't true. They encourage their children to destroy both humans and Arcadians."

"Because we have vowed to stop them and their Slayers, they hate us and have sworn to kill us and our families. In short, we are at war with one another."

Channon sat quietly as she absorbed that last bit. So that was the eternal struggle he'd mentioned yesterday. "Is that why you are here?"

This time the anguish in his eyes was so severe that she winced from it. "No. I'm here because I made a promise."

"About what?"

He didn't answer, but she felt the rigidness return to his body. He was a man in pain, and she wondered why.

But then she figured it out. "The Katagaria destroyed your family, didn't they?"

"They took everything from me." The agony in his voice was so raw, so savage.

Never in her life had she heard anything like it.

Channon wanted to soothe him in a way she'd never

wanted to soothe anyone else. She wished she could erase the past and return his family to him.

Seeking to distract him, she went back to the prior topic. "If you're at war with each other, do you have armies?"

He shook his head. "Not really. We have Sentinels, who are stronger and faster than the rest of our species. They are the designated protectors of both man and were-kind."

Reaching up, she touched his mask that covered the tattoo on his face. "Do all Arcadians have your markings?"

Sebastian looked away. "No. Only Sentinels have them."

She smiled at the knowledge. "You're a Sentinel."

"I *was* a Sentinel."

The stress on the past tense told her much. "What happened?"

"It was a long time ago, and I'd rather not talk about it."

She could respect that, especially since he'd already answered so much. But her curiosity about it was almost more than she could bear. Still, she wouldn't pry. "Okay, but can I ask one more thing?"

"Sure."

"When you say long ago, I have a feeling that takes on a whole new meaning. Was it a decade or two, or—"

"Two hundred fifty-four years ago."

Her jaw dropped. "Have you been alone all this time?"

He nodded.

Her chest drew tight at that. Two hundred years alone. She couldn't imagine it. "And you have no one?"

Sebastian fell silent as old memories surged. He did his best not to remember his role of Sentinel. His family.

He'd been raised to hold honor next to his heart, and with one fatal mistake, he had lost everything he'd ever cared for. Everything he'd once been.

"I was . . . banished," he said, the word sticking in his throat. He'd never once in all this time uttered the word aloud. "No Arcadian is allowed to associate with me."

"Why would they banish you?"

He didn't answer.

Instead, he pointed in front of them. "Look up, Channon. I think there's something over there you'll find far more interesting than me."

Seriously doubting that, Channon turned her head, then gaped. On the hill far above was a large wooden hall surrounded by a group of buildings. Even from this distance, she could make out people and animals moving about.

She blinked, unable to believe her eyes. "Oh my God," she breathed. "It's a real Saxon village!"

"Complete with bad hygiene and no plumbing."

Her heart hammered as they approached the hill at a slow and steady speed. "Can't you make this thing move any faster?" she asked, eager to get a closer view.

"I can, but they will view it as a sign of aggression and might decide to shoot a few arrows into us."

"Oh. Then I can wait. I don't want to be a pincushion."

Sebastian remained silent and watched her as she strained to see more of the town. He smiled at her exuberance as she twisted in the saddle, her hips brushing painfully against his swollen groin.

After the night they had shared, it amazed him just how much he longed to possess her again, how much his body craved hers.

He still couldn't believe he'd told her as much as he had about his past and people, yet as his mate, she had a right to know all about him.

If she would be his mate.

He still hadn't really made up his mind about that.

The kindest thing would be to return her and let her go. But he didn't want to. He missed having someone to care for and someone who cared for him.

How many times had he lain awake at night aching for a family again? Wishing for the comfort of a soothing touch? Missing the sound of laughter and the warmth of friendship?

For centuries, his solitude had been his hell.

And this woman sitting in his lap would be his only salvation.

If he dared . . .

Channon bit her lip as they entered the bailey and she saw real, live Saxon people at work in the village. There were men laying stone, rebuilding a portion of the gate. Women with laundry and foodstuffs walking around, talking amongst themselves. And children! Lots of Saxon children were running around, laughing and playing games with each other.

Better still, there were merchants and music, acrobats, and jongleurs. "Is there a festival going on?"

He nodded. "The harvest is in and there's a celebration all week long to mark it."

She struggled to understand what the crowd around them said.

It was incredible! They were speaking Old English!

"Oh, Sebastian," she cried, throwing her arms around him and holding him close. "Thank you for this! Thank you!"

Sebastian clenched his teeth at the sensation of her breasts flattened against him. Of her breath tickling his neck.

His groin tightened even more, and it took all his human powers to leash the beast within. He felt the ripping inside as he set the two halves of him against each other.

It was a dangerous thing he did, but for both their sakes, it was a necessary action. Especially since both halves of him wanted the same thing—they wanted the Claiming where Channon would entrust herself to him, the ceremony that would bind them together for eternity. It wasn't something to be taken lightly. She would have to give up everything to be with him. Everything. And he wasn't sure if he could ask that of her.

It would be unfair to her, and he definitely wasn't worth such a sacrifice.

He saw the happiness in Channon's eyes and smiled at her.

But his smile faded as he looked around the town and saw all the innocent lives that would end if something went wrong.

Bracis had shown a rare streak of intelligence when he had set up this exchange. Sebastian was forbidden by his Sentinel oath to transform into his dragon form or to use his powers in any way that could betray his heritage to the humans. To the innocent, he must always appear human.

Bracis had sworn that the Katagaria would come in as humans to make the exchange and then leave peacefully. Unfortunately, Sebastian had no choice except to trust them.

Of course, Bracis knew the extent of Sebastian's powers, and the Katagari male would be an absolute idiot to cross him. And though the beast could be stupid, Bracis wasn't *that* stupid.

As soon as they reached the stable, Sebastian helped Channon down, then dismounted behind her. He pulled his hauberk lower so that no one could see just how much he craved the woman before him.

Channon watched as Sebastian removed his huge broadsword from his horse and fastened it to the baldric at his waist. She had to admit the man looked delectable like that, so manly and virile.

The chain mail sleeves fell from the shoulders of the leather armor, clinking ever so slightly with his movements. The laces of the hauberk were open, showing a hint of the hairs on his chest, and all too well she remembered her hours of running her fingers and mouth over that lush skin.

And as she stared at the small scar on his neck, she ached to trace it with her tongue. This man had a body and aura that should be cloned and made standard equipment for all men. Prideful and dangerous, it made every female part of her sit up and pant.

Stop that! she snapped at herself. They were in the middle of town and . . .

And she had other people to study.

Yeah right. Like they were really more interesting than Sebastian.

He adjusted his sword so that the hilt came forward and the blade trailed down his leg, then pulled a leather bag from the saddle. A youth ran up to take his mount.

"What day is today?" he asked the boy in Old English.

"It be Tuesday, sir."

Sebastian thanked him and gave him two coins before relinquishing his horse to the boy's care.

He turned toward her. "You ready?"

"Absolutely. I've dreamed of this my whole life."

Channon held her breath as he led her through the bustling village.

Sebastian looked behind him to see Channon as she tried to watch everything at once. She was so happy to be here.

Maybe there was hope for them after all. Maybe bringing her here hadn't been a mistake.

"Tell me, Channon, have you ever eaten Saxon bread?"

"Is it good?"

"The best." Taking her hand, he pulled her into a shop across the dirt road.

Channon breathed in the sweet smell of baking bread as they entered the bakery. Bread was lined up on the wooden counter and in baskets on tables all over the room. An older, heavyset woman stood to the side, trying to move a large sack across the floor.

"Here," Sebastian said, rushing to her side. "Let me get that."

Straightening up, she smiled in gratitude. "Thank you. I need it over there by my workbench."

Sebastian hefted the heavy sack onto his shoulder.

Channon watched, her mouth watering as his hauberk lifted and gave her a flash of his hard, tanned abs. His broad shoulders and toned biceps flexed from the strain. And when he placed the sack on the floor by the bench, she was gifted with a nice view of his rear covered by his black leather pants.

Oh yeah, she'd love a bite of that.

"Now what can I do for you gentle folks?" the woman asked.

"What looks good to you, Channon?"

Was that a trick question or what?

Forcing herself to look at something other than Sebastian, she attempted to find a substitute to sink her teeth into. "What do you recommend?" she asked, trying out her Old English. She'd never used it before in conversation.

To her amazement, the woman understood her. "If you're in the mind for something sweet, I just pulled a honey loaf from the oven."

"That would be wonderful," Channon said.

The woman left them alone. Sebastian stood back while she examined the different kinds of bread in the shop.

"So what's in the bag?" she asked, indicating the black one Sebastian had removed from his horse.

"It's just something I need to take care of. Later."

Again with the hedging. "Is that why you came back here?"

He nodded, but there was something very guarded in his look, one that warned her this topic was quite closed.

The woman returned with the bread and sliced it for them. While Channon ate the warm, delicious slice, the woman asked Sebastian if he would help her move some boxes from a cart outside into the back of her shop.

He left his bag with Channon, then went to help.

Channon listened to them in the other room while she
ate the bread and drank the cider the woman had also
given her. Her gaze fell to the black bag and curiosity got
the better of her. Leaning over, she opened it to see what
it contained. Her breath left her body as she saw the tapestry inside.

He really had stolen it. But why?

The old woman came in, brushing her hands on her
apron. "That's a good man you got there, my lady."

Blushing at being caught in her snooping, Channon
straightened up. At the moment, she wasn't so sure about
that. "Is he still unloading the cart?"

The woman motioned her to the back, then took her to
look out the door. In the alley behind the shops, she saw
Sebastian playing a game with two boys who were wield-
ing wooden swords and shields against him while pre-
tending to be warriors fighting a dragon. The irony of their
game wasn't lost on her.

She took a minute to watch him laughing and teasing
them. The sight warmed her heart.

The Sebastian she had come to know was a man of
many facets. Caring, compassionate, and tender in a way
she'd never known before. Yet there was a savage un-
dercurrent to him, one that let her know he wasn't a man
to be taken lightly.

And as she watched him playing with the children,
something strange happened to her. She wondered what
he would look like playing with his own children.

With their children . . .

She could see the image so plainly that it scared her.

"Why do you wear a mask?" one of the boys asked
him.

"Because I'm not as pretty as you," Sebastian teased.

"I'm not pretty," the little boy said indignantly. "I'm a
handsome boy."

"Handsome you are, Aubrey," a middle-aged man said as he moved a keg through the back door of the building across the way. The man looked to Sebastian.

He gaped widely, then wiped his hand on his shirt and moved to shake Sebastian's arm. "It's been a long time since I seen one of you. It's an honor to shake your arm, sir."

The boys paused in their play. "Who is he, grandfather?"

"He's a dragon slayer, Aubrey, like the ones I tell you about at night when you go to sleep." The man indicated Sebastian's mask and sword. "I was just your age when they came to Lindsey and slew the Megalos."

She wondered if Sebastian was one of the ones who had come that day.

As if sensing her, Sebastian turned his head to see her in the doorway. "If you'll excuse me," he said to the man and boys, then made his way toward her.

Sebastian could tell by Channon's face that something was troubling her. "Is something wrong?"

"Were you one of the ones who fought the Megalos?"

He shook his head as pain sliced through him. If not for his banishment, he would have been here that day. Unlike the other Sentinels, he had to fight the Katagaria alone. "No."

"Oh."

"Is something else wrong? You still don't look happy."

She met his gaze levelly. "You stole the tapestry from the museum," she said in modern English so no one else would understand her. "I want to know why."

"I had to get it back here."

"Why?"

"Because it's the ransom for another Sentinel. If I don't give them the tapestry on Friday, they will kill him."

Channon scowled at that. "Why do they want the tapestry?"

"I have no idea. But since a man's life was at stake, I didn't bother to ask."

Suddenly, she remembered what he'd said last night about the tapestry. *"It was made by a woman named Antiphone back in seventh-century Britain. It's the story of her grandfather and his brother and their eternal struggle between good and evil."*

On their way into town, he'd said it was the story of *his* grandfather.

"Antiphone is your sister?"

"Was my sister. She died a long time ago."

By the look on his face she could tell the loss was still with him.

"Why was her tapestry in the museum?"

"Because . . ." He took a deep breath to stave off the agony inside him, agony so severe that it made his entire being hurt.

He felt the tic working in his jaw as he forced himself to answer her question. "The tapestry was with her when she died. I tried to return it to my family, but they wanted nothing to do with me. I couldn't stand having it around me, so I took it into the future where I knew someone would preserve it and make sure it was honored and protected as she should have been."

"You plan on taking it back after all this is over with, don't you?"

He frowned at her astuteness. "How did you know?"

"I would say I'm psychic, but I'm not. I just figured a man with a heart as big as yours wouldn't just steal something without making amends."

"You don't know me that well."

"I think I do."

Sebastian clenched his teeth. No, she didn't know. He wasn't a good man. He was fool.

If not for him, Antiphone would have lived. Her death had been all his fault. It was a guilt that he lived with constantly. One that would never cease, never heal.

And in that moment he realized something. He had to let Channon go. There was no way he could keep her. There was no way he could share his life with her.

If anything should ever happen to her . . .

It would be his fault, too. As his mate, she would be prime Katagari bait. Even though he was banished, he was still a Sentinel, and his job was to seek and destroy every Slayer he could find.

Alone he could fight them. But without his patria to guard Channon while he fulfilled his ancient oath, there was always a chance she would end up as Antiphone had.

He would sooner spend the rest of his life celibate than let that happen.

Celibate! No!

He squelched the rebellious scream of the inner Drakos. For the next three weeks, he would guard her life with his own, and once his mark was gone from her, he would take her home.

It was what *had* to be done.

*After they left the bakery, they spent the afternoon brows-*ing the stalls and sampling the food and drink.

Channon couldn't believe this day. It was the best one of her entire life. And it wasn't just because she was in Saxon Britain, it was because she had Sebastian by her side. His light teasing and easy-going manner wrapped around her heart and made her ache to keep him.

"Beg pardon, my lord?"

They turned to find a man standing behind them while they were watching an acrobat.

"Aye?" Sebastian asked.

"I was told by His Majesty, King Henfrith, to come and ask for the honor of your company tonight. He wishes to extend his full and most cordial hospitality to you and to your lady."

Channon felt giddy. "I get to meet a king?"

Sebastian nodded. "Tell His Majesty that it would be my honor to meet with him. We shall be along shortly."

The messenger left.

Channon breathed nervously. "I don't know about this. Am I dressed appropriately?"

"Yes, you are. I assure you, you will be the most beautiful woman there." Then, her gallant champion offered her his arm. Taking it, she let him lead her through town to the large hall.

As they drew near the hall's door, she could hear the music and laughter from inside as the people ate their supper. Sebastian opened the door and allowed her to enter first.

Channon hesitated in the doorway as she looked around in awe. It was more splendid than anything she'd ever imagined.

A lord's table was set apart from the others, and there were three women and four men seated there. The man with the crown she assumed was the king, the lady at his right, his queen, and the others must be the daughters and sons or some other dignitaries perhaps.

Servants bustled around with food while dogs milled about, catching scraps from the diners. The music was sublime.

"Nervous?" Sebastian asked her in modern English.

"A little. I have no idea what Saxon etiquette is."

He lifted her hand to his lips and kissed her fingers, causing a warm chill to sweep through her. "Follow my lead, and I will show you everything you need to know to live in my world."

She cocked her brow at his words. There was something hidden in that. She was sure of it. "You are going to take me home at the next full moon, right?"

"I gave you my word, my lady. That is the one thing I have never broken, and I most assuredly would not break my oath to you."

"Just checking."

A hush fell over the crowd as they crossed the room and neared the lord's table.

Channon swallowed nervously. But she was there with the most handsome man in the kingdom. Dressed in his black armor and mask, Sebastian was a spectacularly masculine sight. The man had a regal presence that promised strength, speed, and deadly precision.

He stopped before the table and gave a low, courtly bow. Channon gave what she hoped was an acceptable curtsy.

"Greetings, Your Majesty," Sebastian said, straightening. "I am Sebastian Kattalakis, a Prince of Arcadia."

Channon's jaw went slack with that declaration. A prince? Was he for real or was it another joke?

He turned to her, his features guarded. "My lady, Channon."

The king rose to his feet and bowed to them. "Your Highness, it has been a long time since I've had the privilege of a dragon slayer's company. I owe your house more than I can ever repay. Please, come and be seated in honor. You and your lady-wife are welcomed here for as long as you wish to stay."

Sebastian led Channon to the table and sat her to his right, beside a man who introduced himself as the king's son-in-law.

"Are you really a prince?" she whispered to Sebastian.

"A most disinherited one, but yes. My grandfather, Lycaon, was the King of Arcadia."

"Oh my God," Channon said as pieces of history came together in her mind. "The king cursed by Zeus?"

"And the Fates."

Lycanthrope, the Greek word for werewolves, vampires, and shape-shifters, was taken from Lycaon, the King of Arcadia. Stunned, she wondered what other so-called myths and legends were actually real.

"You know, you are better than the Rosetta stone to a historian."

Sebastian laughed. "Glad to know I have some use to you."

More than he knew—and it wasn't just the knowledge he held. Today was the only day she could recall in an exceptionally long time when she hadn't been lonely. Not once. She'd enjoyed every minute of this day and didn't really want it to end.

She looked forward to spending the next few weeks with Sebastian in his world. And deep inside where she best not investigate was a part of her that wondered if, when the time came, she'd be able to leave him.

How could a woman give up a man who made her feel the way Sebastian did every time he looked at her?

She wasn't sure it was possible.

Sebastian cut and served her from the roast of something she couldn't quite identify. Thinking it best not to ask, she took a bite and discovered it was quite good.

They ate in silence while others finished their meals and started dancing.

After a time, Channon glanced to Sebastian and noticed his eyes seemed troubled. "Are you all right?" she asked.

Sebastian ran his hand over the uncovered portion of his face. He felt ill inside. The harmony between his two halves had been disrupted by his inner fighting over Channon, and the pain of it was almost more than he could stand.

The Drakos wanted her regardless, but the man in him refused to see her endangered. The struggle between the two sides was so severe that he wondered how he was going to make it for the next three weeks without doing permanent damage to one or the other of his halves.

It was this kind of internal struggle that caused the madness in their youth. And if he didn't restore the balance soon, his powers would be permanently scarred.

"Jet lag from the time-jump," he said.

Forcing the dragon back into submission, he didn't speak to Channon while she ate. He allowed her the time to experience the life and beauty of this time without intruding on her.

Gods, how he ached to make her stay here. He could take her right now and bind her to him for the rest of his life. It was fully within his power.

But he couldn't do that to her. The man in him refused to claim her against her will. It had to be her choice. He would never accept anything less than that.

Channon frowned as she noted the seriousness in Sebastian's eyes. "Are you sure you're all right?" she asked.

"I'm fine. Really."

She still didn't buy that. The musicians paused and the crowd clapped for them. As she applauded the musicians and dancers, Channon became aware of something on her hand. Frowning, she studied her palm. "What in the world?"

Sebastian swallowed. Up until now he'd used his powers to shield her from the marking. But his powers were weakening . . .

She tried to rub it off. "What is this?"

He started to tell her the truth, but it wedged in his throat. She didn't need to know that. Not right now. He didn't want to destroy the fun she was having by interjecting such a serious topic. "It's from the time-jump," he lied. "It's nothing major."

"Oh," Channon said, dropping her hand. "Okay."

The musicians started up again. Sebastian excused himself from her.

Channon frowned. Something in his demeanor concerned her.

He walked too deliberately with his spine rigid and his shoulders back.

Following after him, she watched as he left the hall and went outside. He rounded the side of the hall and headed toward a small well.

Channon stayed back while he pulled water from the

well, then removed his mask and splashed the water over his face.

"Sebastian?" she asked softly, moving to his side. "Tell me what's wrong with you."

Sebastian raked his gloved hands through his hair, dampening it. "I'm okay, really."

"You keep saying that, but . . ."

She placed her hand on his arm. The sensation of her touch rocked him so fiercely that he wanted to growl from it. His body reacted viciously as desire tore through him.

The dragon snarled and circled, demanding her. *Take her. Take her. Take her.*

No! He would not cost her her life. He would not endanger her.

"I shouldn't have brought you here, Channon," he said as he turned his powers inward to harness the Drakos. "I'm sorry."

She smiled at him. "Don't be. It's not turning out so badly. It's actually kind of nice here."

He shut his eyes and turned away. He had to. The beast inside was snarling again. Salivating.

Claim her.

It wanted total possession.

And so did the man.

His groin tightened even more, and he wondered how much longer he could keep that part of him leashed.

Channon saw the feral look in his eyes as he raked a ravenous look over her. Her body reacted to it with a desire so powerful that it stunned and scared her. She wanted him to look at her like that. Forever.

His breathing ragged, he cupped her face in his hands and pulled her close for a fierce kiss. Channon moaned at the raw passion she tasted as she surrendered her weight to him.

She wrapped her arms around his neck and felt his muscles bunch and flex. Images of last night tore through her. Again she could see his naked body moving in the moonlight and feel him deep and hard inside her.

Sebastian growled at the taste of her, at the feel of her tongue sweeping against his. Out of his mind with the passion, he pinned her against the wall of the gate.

He wanted her no matter the consequences, no matter the time or place.

Channon felt his erection as he held her between him and the wall. As if magnetized, her hips brushed against him. She wanted to feel him inside her again. She wanted nothing between them except bare skin.

"What is it you do to me?" she breathed.

Sebastian pulled back as her words penetrated the haziness of his mind. Still, all he could smell was Channon. Her scent spun around his head, making him even dizzier. He dipped his head for her lips, then barely caught himself.

Hissing, he forced himself to release her. If he kissed her again, he would take her here in the yard like an animal, without regard to her humanity, without regard for her choice.

Claiming was a special moment, and he refused to sully it like the Katagari. No, he wouldn't take her like this. Not out here where anyone could see them. He would not let the Drakos win.

"Channon," he whispered. "Please, go back inside."

Channon started to refuse, but the steeliness in his body kept her from it. "Okay," she said.

She paused at the corner of the hall and looked back at him. He was now leaning over the well with his head hung low. She didn't know what was wrong, but she was sure it wasn't good.

"Ha, take that!"

Channon turned at the sound of a child laughing. She saw the two boys with wooden swords who had been fighting Sebastian earlier. They ran across the yard.

"I will kill you, nasty dragon," one boy cried as they ran into a forge where the blacksmith cursed and chased them out, telling the tallest that he should be home eating.

She shook her head. Some things never changed, no matter the time period. Curious about what else reminded her of home, she crossed the yard.

Sebastian breathed deeply, trying to summon his powers back to him. This was not good. If he stayed around Channon, by the time Friday arrived, he wouldn't be able to face the Katagaria trio.

He had to have his powers back, intact and strong, which meant that he would either have to claim her or find some place safe for her to stay so that he could get distance from her.

Because if he didn't, they would both die.

"Bas?"

Sebastian looked around the yard, trying to find the source of that whispered call. It was a nickname no one had used in centuries.

Gold flashed to his right. To his shock, Damos appeared, then collapsed on the ground. Like a wounded animal, his brother held himself on all fours with his head hung low.

Unable to believe his eyes, Sebastian went to him. "Damos?"

Damos lifted his head to look at him. Instead of the hatred and disgust he expected to see, Sebastian saw only pain and guilt. "Did you get the tapestry?"

Sebastian couldn't answer as he saw his brother's face again. The two of them were almost identical in build and looks. The only real difference was in their hair color. Sebastian's hair was black while Damos's was a dark reddish-brown.

And as Sebastian looked into those eyes that were the same color as his own, the past flashed through his mind.

"You're nothing but a cowardly traitor. You've never been worth anything. I wish it had been you they tore

apart. If there were any justice, it would be you lying in the grave and not Antiphone." The cruel words echoed in his head, and even now he could feel the bite of the whip as they delivered the two hundred lashes to his back.

Battered and bloody, Sebastian had been dumped in a cesspit and left there to die or survive as he saw fit.

He'd crawled from the pit and somehow found his way into the woods, where he'd lain for days floating in and out of consciousness. To this day, he wasn't sure how he'd survived it.

"Bas!" Damos snapped, wincing from the effort as he pushed himself slowly to his feet. He staggered, and against his will, Sebastian found himself helping his brother to the well where he propped him.

Damos's long reddish-brown hair was lank and clotted with blood and snarls. His face was battered and his clothes torn. "You look like hell."

"Yeah, well, it's hard to look good when you're being tortured."

Sebastian knew that firsthand. "You escaped?"

He nodded. "Where's the tapestry?"

"It's safe."

Damos locked gazes with him. "Were you really going to trade it for me?"

"I brought it here, didn't I?"

Tears gathered in Damos's eyes as he looked at him. "I am so sorry for what I did to you."

Sebastian was stunned. So, Damos did know what an apology was.

"The Katagaria told me what happened that day, how they tricked you." Damos placed his hand against the scar on Sebastian's neck that Sebastian had received while trying to save Antiphone's life. "I can't believe you survived them. And I can't believe you did this for me."

"Not like I had anything better to do."

Damos hissed and placed his hand to his eyes. "Those damned feelers. They're trying to find me."

Sebastian went cold. Without his powers, he couldn't sense the feelers, but if they were sending them out for Damos, then they would find . . .

Channon!

His heart pounding, he ran for the hall.

Channon wished she had her notepad to take notes on everything she saw. This was just incredible!

Enchanted, she walked idly past the stalls and huts, looking inside to see families eating and spending the evening together.

"You look lost."

She turned at the voice behind her. There were three men there, handsome all and quite tall. "Not lost," she offered. "Just out for a bit of fresh air."

The blond man appeared to be the leader of the small group. "You know, that can be quite dangerous for a woman alone."

Channon frowned as a wave of panic washed over her. "I beg your pardon?"

"Tell me, Acmenes." The blonde spoke to the tall brunette beside him. "Why do you think an Arcadian would bring a human woman through time?"

Panic gone, sheer terror set in, especially since the man was speaking in modern English.

She tried to head back to Sebastian, but of the third man caught her. He grabbed her right hand and showed it to his friends. "Because she's his mate."

The one called Acmenes laughed. "How precious is this? An Arcadian with a human dragonswan."

"No," the brunette said, "it's better. A lone Sentinel with a human mate."

They laughed cruelly.

Channon glared. She might look harmless, but she'd been on her own for quite some time, and as a woman alone, she'd learned a few things.

Tae Kwon Do was one of them. She caught the man holding her with her elbow and twisted out of his grasp. Before the others could reach her, she ran for the hall.

Unfortunately, the Katagaria moved a lot faster than she did and they grabbed her before she could reach it.

"Let her go." Sebastian's voice rolled across the yard like dangerous thunder as he unsheathed his sword.

"Oh no," Acmenes said sarcastically. "This is the best of all. A Sentinel who has *lost* his powers."

Channon's heart clenched at their words.

Sebastian's smile was taunting, wicked. "I don't need my powers to defeat you."

Before she could blink, the Katagaria attacked Sebastian.

"Run, Channon," Sebastian said as he delivered a staggering blow to the first one who reached him.

Channon didn't go far. She couldn't leave him to fight the men alone. Not that he appeared to need any help. She watched as they attacked him at once and he deftly knocked them back.

"Um, Acmenes," the youngest Katagari said as he picked himself up from the ground and panted. "He's kicking our butts."

Acmenes laughed. "Only in human form."

In a brilliant flash, Acmenes transformed into a dragon. The crowd that had gathered at the start of the fight shrieked and ran chaotically for shelter.

Channon stumbled back.

Standing at least twenty feet high, Acmenes was a terrifying sight. His green and orange scales shimmered in the fading daylight while his blue wings flapped. He slung his spiked tail around, but Sebastian flipped out of the way.

The other two flashed into dragon form.

Sebastian held his sword tightly in his hands as he faced them. Even if he still held his powers unsevered, he wouldn't have been able to transform. Not while in the middle of a human village. It was forbidden.

Damn you, Fates.

"What's the matter, Kattalakis?" Acmenes asked. "Won't you breech your oath to protect your humans?"

Bracis laughed. "He can't, brother, his powers are too fragmented. He's powerless to stop us."

Acmenes shook his large, scaled head and sighed. "This is so anticlimactic. All these years you've chased us, and now . . ." He tsked. "To comfort you as you die, Sebastian, know that your dragonswan will be as well used by all of us as your sister was."

Raw agony ripped through Sebastian.

Over and over, he saw his sister's face and felt her blood on his skin as he held her lifeless body in his arms and wept.

"Kill him," Acmenes said. Then he turned toward Channon.

The dragon beast inside Sebastian roared with needful vengeance. He'd been unable to save Antiphone, but he would never let Channon die. Not like that.

Ceding his humanity, he let loose his shields. His change came so swiftly that he didn't even feel it. All he felt was the love in his heart for his mate, the animal desperation to keep her safe regardless of law or sense.

Channon froze at the sight of Sebastian's dragon form. The same height as Acmenes, his scales were bloodred and black. He looked like some fierce, terrifying menace, and she searched for something to remind her of the man he'd been two seconds ago.

She found none of him.

What she did see terrified her.

Acmenes swung about to face Sebastian as he savagely attacked the other two dragons. Fire shot through the village as they fought like the primeval beasts they were.

Then, to her horror, she saw Sebastian kill the dragon on his left with one sharp bite. The one on his right stumbled away from him in wounded pain, then took to the skies.

Acmenes reached for her, but Sebastian tackled him. The force of them hitting the ground shook it. They fought like men, slugging at each other, and yet like dragons, as their tails coiled and moved trying to sting one another.

She cringed as both dragons were wounded countless times by their fighting, but neither would pull back. She'd never seen anything like it. They were locked in the throes of a blood feud.

Acmenes hefted his body and threw Sebastian over his head, then rolled to his monstrous feet. He stumbled as he tried to reach the sky, but before he could leap, Sebastian caught him through the heart with his tail.

"Dragon!"

Now armed and prepared, the men of the village came running back to do damage to the creatures who had invaded them.

At first Channon thought they came to help Sebastian, until she realized that they intended to attack him.

Without thought, she went to him. "Run, Sebastian," she said.

He didn't. He turned on her with frightening eyes, and in that moment she realized the man she knew was not in that body.

The dragon snarled at her as the crowd attacked him. Throwing his head back, he shrieked.

To her shock, he didn't attack the people.

Instead, he grabbed her in his massive claw and took flight.

Channon screamed as she watched the ground drift far away from her. She had no idea where he was taking her, but she didn't like this. Not even a little bit.

"Sebastian?"

Sebastian heard Channon's voice. But it came from a distance. He could only vaguely remember her.

Vaguely recall . . .

He shrieked as something flew past his head. Looking behind him, he saw Bracis coming for them.

And with the sight, his human memories came flooding back.

"Sebastian, help us. We're trapped by the Slayers."

"I can't, Percy. I can't leave Antiphone."

"She's safe in the hills. We are in the open, unprotected. Please, Sebastian. I'm too young to die. Please don't let them kill me. I know you can beat them. Please, please help me."

And so he had heeded the mental distress call and gone to protect his young cousin and brother, never knowing Percy's cry for help had been a trick, never knowing that Percy had deliberately summoned him from the cave.

He'd found his cousin barely alive and learned too late they had forced Percy to call for him.

By the time he'd returned to the cave where he'd left his sister hiding, the Slayers were gone.

And so was his sister's life.

Devastated on a level he'd never known existed, he'd refused to speak up in his own defense when his people had banished him.

He'd offered no argument at all against Damos's insults.

He should never have left Antiphone unprotected.

Now he looked at the woman he held cradled in his palm.

Channon.

The Fates had entrusted this woman to him, just as his brother had entrusted Antiphone to him.

He would not let Bracis have her. This time, he would see her safe. No matter what it cost him, she would live.

Sebastian headed for the forest.

Channon held her breath as they landed on the ground in a small clearing.

"Hide." The word seemed to sizzle out of Sebastian's dragon mouth.

She went without question, running into the trees and underbrush, looking for someplace safe. The forest was so thick that she quickly lost sight of the dragons. But she could hear them as they fought. She could feel the ground under her shake.

Grateful for the green dress, she found a clump of bushes and crawled into them to wait and to pray.

*Sebastian circled around Bracis, enjoying the moment, en-*joying the feel of the dragon blood coursing through his veins. For two hundred and fifty years he had dreamed of this moment. He had dreamed of drinking from the fount of vengeance.

Now the moment was upon him.

Bracis was the last of the Slayers left from that day. One by one, Sebastian had hunted them all down. He had hunted them through time and even space itself.

"Are you ready to die?" Sebastian asked his opponent.

Bracis attacked. Sebastian caught him with his teeth and clamped down on the Katagari's shoulder. He tasted the blood of the beast as Bracis shredded at his back with his claws.

Sebastian barely felt it. But what he did feel was the fear inside Bracis. It swelled up with a pungent odor so foul that it made Sebastian laugh.

"You may kill me," Bracis rasped. "But I'm taking you with me."

Something stung Sebastian's shoulder. Snarling, he jerked his head around to see the dagger protruding from his back. But it wasn't the steel that stung; it was the poison that coated the blade. Dragon's Bane.

Roaring from the pain of it, he turned back and finished Bracis off quickly by breaking his long, scaled neck.

He stood over the body of his enemy, staring at it blankly. After all this time, he'd wanted more out of the kill. He'd expected it to release the agony in his heart, to relieve his guilt.

It didn't.

He felt nothing except disappointed by it. Cheated.

No. In two hundred and fifty years only one thing had ever given him a moment's worth of peace.

Suddenly, a scream tore through the woods.

Channon.

Sebastian reared up to his full twenty foot height, searching for her through the trees with his dragon sight and senses.

He heard nothing more. His heart pounding, he ran for the woods where she'd vanished. With every step that closed the distance between them, all his feelings rushed through him. He relived every moment of Antiphone's death.

The guilt, the fear, the raw agony.

Under the onslaught of his human feelings, the dragon inside him receded again, leaving only the man. The man who had been crushed that day. The man who had sworn over his sister's grave to never let another person into his heart.

The same man who had looked into a pair of crystal blue eyes over dinner one night and had seen a future inside them that he wanted to live. A future with laughter and love. One spent in quiet serenity with a woman standing beside him to keep him strong and grounded.

Leaves and brambles tore at his flesh, but he paid no attention to them.

Like Antiphone, he'd left Channon alone to face an untold nightmare.

Left her to face . . .

He came to a stop as he caught sight of her.

Frowning, Sebastian struggled to breathe. His vision was so blurry from the poison that he wasn't sure he could trust it.

He blinked and blinked again. And still it stayed before his eyes. Channon stood with a sword in her hand, and it was angled at Damos's throat.

"Bas, would you please tell her I'm not a Katagari."

Channon glanced over her shoulder to see Sebastian standing naked in the woods. Human once more, he was pale and covered in sweat.

"Let him go."

By the sound of Sebastian's voice, she knew the man she held hadn't been lying to her. He was one of the good guys.

The instant she saw Sebastian stumble, she dropped the sword she'd taken from this stranger.

Channon ran to his side. "Sebastian?"

He was shaking in her arms. Together, they sank to the ground and she held his head in her lap.

"I thought you were dead," he whispered, running his hand over her forearms. "I heard you scream."

The man she'd cornered knelt beside them. "I startled her. I was trying to help you with Bracis. I sent out a feeler for your essence and it led me to her. You didn't tell me you were mated."

Channon ignored the man as Sebastian's body temperature dropped alarmingly.

Why was Sebastian trembling so? His wounds didn't look that severe. "Sebastian, what's wrong with you?

"Dragon's Bane."

Channon frowned as the man cursed. What was Dragon's Bane?

"Sebastian," he said forcefully, taking Sebastian's face in his hands and forcing him to look up at him. "Don't you dare die on me. Damn you, fight this."

"I'm already dead to you, Damos," he said, his voice ragged as he turned away from him. "You told me to die painfully."

Sebastian closed his eyes.

Channon saw the grief in Damos's eyes as her own tore through her. This couldn't be happening. She wanted to wake up.

But it wasn't a nightmare, it was real.

Damos looked at her, his greenish-gold eyes searing her

with power and emotion. "He's going to die unless you help him."

"What can I do?"

"Give him a reason to live."

Her hand started to tingle where the mark was. Channon scowled as it began to fade. "What the . . . ?"

"We're losing him. When he dies, your mark will be gone, too."

The reality of the moment hit her ferociously. Sebastian was going to die?

No, it couldn't be.

"Sebastian?" she said, shaking him. "Can you hear me?"

He shifted ever so slightly in her arms.

She wouldn't let him go like this. She couldn't. Though they had only known each other one day, it felt as if they'd been together an eternity. The thought of losing him crippled her.

"Sebastian, do you remember what you said to me in the hotel room? You said, 'I'm here because I know the sadness inside you. I know what it feels like to wake in the morning, lost and lonely and aching for someone to be there with me.' "

She pressed her lips against his cheek and wept. "I don't want to be alone anymore, Sebastian. I want to wake up with you like I did this morning. I want to feel your arms around me, your hand in my hair."

He went limp in her arms.

"No!" Channon cried, holding him close to her heart. "Don't you do this to me, Sebastian Kattalakis. Don't you dare make me believe in knights in shining armor, in men who are good and decent, and then leave me alone again. Damn it, Sebastian. You promised to take me home. You promised not to leave me."

The mark faded from her palm.

Channon wept as her heart splintered. Until that moment, she hadn't realized that against all known odds, against all known reason, she loved this man.

And she didn't want to lose him.

She pressed her wet cheek to his lips. "I love you, Sebastian. I just wished you'd lived long enough for us to see what could become of us."

Suddenly, she felt another tingle in her palm. It grew to a burning itch. It was followed by a slow, tiny stirring of air against her cheek.

Damos expelled a deep breath. "That's it, little brother. Fight for your mate. Fight for your dragonswan."

Channon looked up as Damos doffed his cloak, then wrapped it around Sebastian's body.

"Is he going to live?"

"I don't know, but he's trying to. The Fates willing, he will."

Three

Channon bathed Sebastian's fevered brow while she prayed for his survival and whispered for him to come back to her.

After they had stabilized Sebastian, Damos had taken them to a small village in Sussex where humans and Arcadians lived and worked together. She learned that though Arcadians could only time-jump during a full moon, they could use their magic to make lateral jumps from one place to another in the same time frame any time they wanted to.

It didn't really make sense to her, but she didn't care. At the moment, all that mattered to her was the fact that Sebastian was still fighting his way back from death.

It was long after midnight now. They were alone in a large room where the only light came from three candles set in an iron fixture against the wall. Sebastian lay draped in a sheet on an ornate bed that bore the images of dragons and wheat and was shielded from drafts by shimmery white drapes.

The sounds of the night drifted in from the open window while she waited for some sign that he would wake up.

None came.

At some point before dawn, exhaustion overtook her and she curled up by his side and went to sleep.

"Channon?"

Channon felt as if she were floating, as if she had no real form at all.

Suddenly, she stood in a summer field with wildflowers all around her. She was dressed in a sheer, white gown that left her all but bare. There was a medieval castle in the distance, highlighted against the horizon. It reminded her of one of the manuscript pages she studied.

None of it seemed real until she felt strong arms wrap around her.

Glancing over her shoulder, she looked up to find Sebastian behind her. Like her, he was practically naked, dressed only in a pair of thin white pants. The breeze stirred his dark hair around his handsome face, and he flashed those killer dimples. Her heart soaring, she turned in his arms, reached up, and placed her marked palm over his Sentinel tattoo. "Am I dreaming?"

"Yes. This was the only way I could reach you."

She frowned. "I don't understand."

"I'm dying."

"No," she said emphatically, "you're still alive. You came back to me."

The tenderness on his face as he looked at her made her heart pound. "In part, but I still lack the strength I need to wake."

He sat down on the ground and pulled her down with him. "I missed you today."

So had she, in a way that made no sense whatsoever to her, but then feelings seldom do. The entire time he'd been unconscious, she had felt as if a vital part of her was gone.

Now, in the circle of his arms, leaning back against him, she felt right again. She felt whole and warm.

Sebastian took her hand into his and used his thumb to toy gently with her fingers.

"I can't lose you," she whispered. "I've spent hours thinking of my life at home. It was lonely and empty. I had no one to laugh with."

He placed his lips against her temple and kissed her tenderly. Then he cupped her head in his hands and leaned his forehead against her. "I know, love. I've spent my life alone in caves, my only company the sound of the wind outside. But the only way I can fight my way back to you is to regain my powers."

"Regain them how? How did you lose them?"

She felt his lips moving against her skin as he whispered the words while he nuzzled her. It was wonderful to have him holding her again. "I was using them against myself. I set the dragon and the human inside me at odds."

His touch burned through her. She didn't want to live another day without feeling him by her side, without seeing that devilish smile and those deep dimples.

In short, she needed this man.

"Why did you do that?" she asked.

He pulled back and kissed her fingertips. "To protect you."

"From what?"

"Me," he said simply.

Channon stared up at him, baffled by his words. He would never hurt her. She knew that. Even in his true dragon form he had done nothing but protect her. "I don't understand."

He ran his thumb over her palm, tracing the lines of her mark. Chills swept up her arm, tightening her breasts as she watched him.

When he met her gaze, she saw his sorrow. "I lied to you when you asked me about the mark on your hand. Part of the curse of my people is that we are only designated one mate for our entire existence, a mate we don't choose."

Channon frowned. Damos had refused to speak to her when she asked him what he meant when he had called her Sebastian's mate. He'd told her it was for Sebastian to do.

Sebastian kissed her marked palm. "The moment we Arcadians and Katagaria are born, the Fates choose a mate for us. We spend the rest of our lives trying to find our other half. Unlike humans, we can't have a family or children with anyone other than our mate. If we fail to find our other half, we are doomed to live out our lives alone.

"As a human, you have the freewill to love anyone. You can love more than once. But I can't. You, Channon, are the only woman in any time or place who I can love. The only woman I can ever have a family with. The only woman I will ever desire."

She remembered Plato's theory about the human race being two halves of the same person—the male and female who were separated by the gods. Now she realized Plato's theory was based on the reality of Sebastian's people, not hers.

"So what do you need to regain your powers?"

He fingered her lips and stared at her with desperate need. She knew he was still holding himself back, still keeping himself from kissing her.

"You have to claim me as your mate," he said quietly. "Sex regenerates our powers. It heightens them. I was trying so hard to keep from forcing you into the Claiming that I buried them too deeply. There is a delicate balance in all Arcadians and Katagaria between the human and animal half. I was fighting myself so hard to protect you that I ruptured the balance."

"It can only be repaired by Claiming me?"

He nodded.

"And this Claiming, what is it exactly?"

He traced the line of her jaw, making her burn from the inside out. "When you Claim me, you acknowledge me as your soulmate. The ceremony is really quite simple. You place your marked palm over mine and then you take me into your body. You hold me there and say, 'I accept you as you are, and I will always hold you close to my heart. I will walk beside you forever.' "

"And then?"

"I repeat the words back to you."

That seemed just a little too easy to her. If that was all there was to it, why had he fought it so hard? "That's it?"

He hesitated.

Inwardly, she groaned. "I know that look," she said, pulling back slightly from him. "Any time you're not telling me the whole truth you get that look."

He smiled at her and planted a chaste kiss on her cheek. "All right, there is something more. When we join, my natural instinct will be to bond you to me."

That still didn't sound so bad. "Bond me how?"

"With blood."

"Okay, I don't like this part. What do you mean *with blood?*"

He dropped his hands and leaned back on them to watch her. "You know how humans will bind themselves together as blood brothers?"

"Yes."

"It's basically the same thing—but with one major difference. If you take my blood into you, our mortal lives are completely conjoined."

"Meaning we will become one person?" she asked.

"No, nothing like that. Do you remember your Greek myths at all?"

"Some of them."

"Do you remember who Atropos is?"

She shook her head. "Nope, not a clue."

"She is one of the Moirae, the Fates. She's the one who assigns our mates to us at birth, and if we chose to bond with that mate, her sister Clotho, who is the spinner of our lives, combines our life-threads together. At the end of a normal life Atropos will cut the thread and cause a death. But if we are bonded together and our threads are one, then she can't cut one without the other."

"We die together."

"Exactly."

Wow, that was a big commitment. Especially for him. "So you will have a human life span."

"No. My thread is stronger. You will have an Arcadian life span."

She blinked at that. "Are you saying I could live several hundred years?"

He nodded. "Or we could both die tomorrow."

"Whoa. Is there anything else?" she asked, curiously. "Will I also get some of your powers? Mind control? Time-walking?"

He laughed at her. "No. Sorry. My powers are tied to my birth and my destiny. Bonding only extends to our life-threads."

Channon smiled as she rose up on her knees, between his legs. She crouched over him, forcing him to lean back farther on his arms as she hovered over him. She bit her lip as she stared at his handsome face, at those lips she was dying to taste.

"So, what you're offering me is a gorgeous, incredibly sexy man who is completely devoted to me for the next few centuries?"

"Yes."

She smiled even wider. "One who can never stray?"

"Never."

She forced him to lie back on the ground as she straddled his waist and leaned forward on her arms so that her face was just a few inches above his. She felt his hard erection through his pants, pressing against her core. How she wanted him. But first she wanted to make sure she understood all the consequences.

"You know," she said, "it's real hard to say no to this. What downside could there possibly be?"

He shifted his hips under hers, making her burn for him as he tucked a stray piece of her hair back behind her ear. Still, he didn't touch her, and she knew he was leaving it all up to her now.

"The Katagaria who want me dead," he said seriously. "They will never cease coming for us, and because I am banished, it will only be the two of us to fight them off. Our children will be Arcadian and not human, and they, too, will have to battle the Katagaria. But most important, you will have to remain here in the Middle Ages."

"Why?"

"Because of the electricity in your time period. Arcadians who are natural animals such as hawks, panthers, wolves, bears, and such can live in your world. If they are accidentally changed, their animal forms are small or normal enough to hide from humans."

"But if you become a dragon, then we have a Godzilla movie."

"Exactly. And in your time period, there are plenty of tasers and electrical devices that can completely incapacitate me. No offense, but I don't relish being someone's science experiment. Been there, done that, and sold the T-shirt for profit."

She sat up straight, still straddling him, as she digested all of this.

The man offered her the deal of a lifetime.

Sebastian watched her carefully. It was taking all his restraint to keep his hands off her when all he wanted to do was make love to her. He'd told her everything. Now it was up to her, and he trembled with the fear that she would leave him.

She took his hands in hers and held them to her waist. "Our babies will be normal, right?"

"Perfectly normal. They will age like human children

with the only exception being that they won't be teenagers until their twenties."

"And that's a drawback?"

He laughed.

"Oh, by the way, you're no longer banished."

Sebastian scowled. "What?"

"While they were torturing Damos, the Katagaria admitted that they had tricked you so they could get the tapestry from Antiphone. But she refused to let them have it."

"Why? What was so important about it?"

"Unfortunately nothing, but they believed that it contained the secret for immortality. It seems Katagaria legend had it that the granddaughter of their creator had placed his secrets into the work she'd created to honor him. They captured Damos, thinking he had it, and when they found out you alone knew where it was, they arranged the bargain with you."

"My sister died for no reason?"

"Sh," she said, placing her hand over his lips. "Just be glad the truth is out and the tapestry is safe. Damos wants to make the past up to you."

Sebastian couldn't believe it. After all this time, his banishment was lifted?

That meant a real home for Channon where she would be safe. A home where their children would be safe.

Channon laid her body down over his and breathed him in. "Which means you're no longer alone, Sebastian. You don't really need me."

"That's not true. I need you more than I've ever needed anything else. My heart was dead until I looked into your eyes."

He cupped her face in his hands. "I want you to Claim me, Channon," he said fiercely. "I want to spend the rest of my life waking up with you in my arms and feeling your hair in my palm."

She choked as he used her words. He'd heard her. "I want you, too."

Laughing, he rolled over with her, pinning her to the ground and letting her feel every hard, wonderful inch of his body.

They kissed each other in a frenzied hurry as they helped one another out of their clothes.

Channon pulled back as their naked bodies slid against each other. "Does it count if we do this in a dream?"

"This isn't really a dream. It's an alternate place."

"You know, you scare me when you talk like that."

He smiled at her. "I have much to teach you about my world."

"And I am willing to learn it all." Channon kissed those delectable lips as she wrapped her bare legs around his. She felt his erection against her hip, and it made her burn with need.

"Are you sure about this?" he asked, nibbling his way along her jaw. "You'll be giving up all your future *Buffy* episodes."

She drew her breath in sharply between her teeth as she thought it over. "I have to tell you, it's a hard decision to make. Watching Spike prance around and be all Spikey, versus a couple hundred years of making love to a Greek god." She clucked her tongue. "What is a woman to do?"

She moaned as he ran his tongue around her ear and whispered, "What can I do to sway your verdict?"

"That's a real good start right there." She sighed as her body erupted into chills and he dipped his head to torment her breast with his hot mouth. "I guess I'll just have to find another pastime to television watching."

"I think I can help you with that." He rolled over again to place her on top of him.

The intensity of his stare scalded her.

"Tradition demands you be in charge of this, my lady. The whole idea behind the Claiming is that the woman places her life and her trust into the hands of her mate.

Once you accept me, the animal inside me will do whatever it takes to keep you safe."

"Like when you turned into a dragon in front of all those people?"

He nodded.

She smiled. "You know it's a pity I didn't know you in third grade. There was this bully—"

He cut her words off with a kiss.

"Mmm," she breathed. "I like that. Now, where were we?"

She nibbled her way down his chin to his chest.

Sebastian growled as she found his nipple and teased it with her tongue and lips. He felt his powers surging again, felt the air around them charging with the force of it.

Channon felt it, too. She moaned as the energy moved around her body, caressing her.

Sebastian held his left hand up. The mark in his palm glowed and shimmered. Looking into his eyes, Channon covered his mark with hers and laced her fingers with his.

Heat engulfed her entire body as she felt something hot and demanding rush through her. She saw the beast in his eyes and the man as he breathed raggedly.

It was the sexiest thing she'd ever beheld.

Arching her back, she lifted her hips and took him deep into her body.

They moaned in unison.

She watched Sebastian's face as she slowly ground herself against him. "Um, I forgot the words."

He laughed as he lifted his hips, driving himself so deep into her that she groaned. "I accept you as you are."

"Oh," she breathed, then remembering what she was doing, she repeated his words. "I accept you as you are."

"And I will always hold you close to my heart."

"Umm, hmmm. I will most definitely hold you close to my heart."

"I will walk beside you forever."

She placed her hand on his chest, over his heart. "I will walk beside you forever."

His eyes turned eerily dark. He reached up with his free hand and cupped her cheek. His voice was a deep, low growl, a cross between the voice of the dragon and the voice of the man. "I accept you as you are, and I will always hold you close to my heart. I will walk beside you forever."

He'd barely finished the words before his teeth grew long and sharp and his eyes darkened to the color of obsidian.

"Sebastian?"

"Don't be afraid," he said as he bared his fangs. "It's the dragon wanting to bond with you, but I have control of it."

"And if I want to bond with you?"

He hesitated. "Do you understand what you're doing?"

Channon paused with him inside her and locked gazes with him. "I've lived alone all my life, Sebastian. I don't want to do it another day."

He sat up, keeping them joined.

Channon hissed at how good he felt as she wrapped her free arm around his waist and he pulled her against him with his.

She lifted her hips, then dropped herself down on him.

"That's it, love, claim me as yours." Sebastian let her ride him slowly as he waited for more of his powers to return. He needed to be in total control for this.

Their marked hands still joined, he held her close to him so that he could feel her heart beating in rapid time to his.

When he was certain his powers were perfectly aligned, he leaned his head forward and sank his teeth gently into her neck.

Channon shivered at the feeling of his hot breath and teeth on her, but oddly enough, there was no pain at all. Instead, it was an erotic pleasure so intense that her entire body exploded into a sensation of colors and sound. Her head fell back as she felt the strength of him moving through her, the smell of him engulfing her. It was electrifying and terrifying.

Her sight grew sharper and clearer, and she felt her teeth elongate.

Growling, she knew instinctively what she was supposed to do. She clutched feverishly at his shoulders, pulling herself up in his arms. Then she leaned forward and sank her teeth into his shoulder.

For an instant, time stood still with them locked together. Channon couldn't breathe as her body and mind joined his in a place she'd never known existed. It was just the two of them. Just their hearts beating, their bodies joining.

Sebastian hissed as he felt their bonding. The air around them sizzled and spun as they came together in an orgasm so intense, so powerful, that they cried out in unison.

Panting and weak from it, he kissed her lips, holding her to him as he felt her teeth recede.

"That was incredible," she said, still clutching him to her.

He smiled. "Too bad it's a one-time thing."

"Really?"

He nodded. "You're fully human again. Except you have a long life ahead of you."

She bit her lip and gave him a hot, promising look. "And my own pet dragon."

"Aye, my lady. And you can pet him any time you want."

She laughed at him. "You know, since the moment I saw you, I keep having this strange feeling that all of this is just some weird dream."

"Well, if it is, I don't want to wake up."

"Neither do I, my love. Neither do I."

Epilogue

Two years later

Channon left the podium, her heart pounding in triumph.
Every historian in the room had been left completely
speechless by the paper and research she had just delivered to them. She'd done the one thing she'd always
wanted to do.

She'd solved the mystery of the tapestry, which now
hung back in the museum.

"Brilliant research, Dr. Kattalakis," Dr. Lazarus said,
shaking her hand as she left the podium. "Completely
ground-breaking. This takes us into a whole new area."

"Thank you."

She tried to step past him, but he cut her off.

"How ever did you find those answers? I mean that
Book of Dragons, you said it was from the Library of
Alexandria. How did you ever find it?"

She looked past his shoulder to see Sebastian leaning

against the wall with his arms folded across his chest, waiting patiently for her. Dressed all in black, he cut a fearsome pose.

Still, she missed seeing him in his armor. Something about the mail over those luscious muscles . . .

She needed to get back home. Real soon.

She returned her attention to Dr. Lazarus and his questions.

The *Book of Dragons* had been her birthday present from Sebastian last year. He said he'd swiped it the day before the fire that burned the ancient library. With that book and Antiphone's tapestry, she had been able to concoct an entire mythology based on his people that was guaranteed to keep any "experts" from ever discovering the truth of the Draki people.

The Arcadian Draki were safe from human curiosity.

"The book was found in an estate sale. I've handed it over to the Richmond Museum." She patted his arm. "Now, if you'll please excuse me?"

She sidestepped him.

But before she could reach Sebastian, Dr. Herter stopped her. "Have you reconsidered coming back to work?"

She shook her head. "No, sir. I told you, I'm retired."

"But after that paper you just delivered—"

"I'm going home." She handed him the pages in her hand. "Publish it and be happy."

Dr. Herter shook his gray head at her. "The Myth of the Dragon. It's a brilliant piece of fiction."

She smiled. "Yes, it is."

As soon as she reached her soulmate, Sebastian wrapped his arms around her and drew her close. "I don't know if you helped us or hurt us with that."

"We can't let the humans know of you. This way, no one will question the tapestry anymore. It's preserved as you originally wanted, and the academic community can stop nosing around for the truth."

She looked up and saw him staring at the tapestry on the museum's wall. Anytime he thought of his sister, he always looked so incredibly sad. "It's a pity the Fates won't let you guys change the past."

He sighed. "I know. But if we try, they make us pay for it tenfold."

She hugged him tightly, then pulled back so they could leave.

"Well," he said, draping his arm over her shoulders as he walked her out of the museum, "tonight's the full moon. Are you ready to go home?"

"Absolutely, Sir Dragon-Knight. But first . . ."

"I know," he said with a long-suffering sigh, "it's the *Buffy* marathon torture that you always put me through whenever we visit here."

She laughed. He'd been very patient with her on their infrequent visits to her time period, where she caught up on all her favorite shows. "Actually, I was thinking there is one thing I do miss most when we're in Sussex."

"And that is?"

"Whipped cream loincloths."

He arched a brow at that, then smiled a wicked smile that flashed his dimples. "Mmm, my lady, I definitely like the way your mind works."

"Glad to hear it, because you know what they say?"

"What's that?" he asked as he opened the door for her.

"Be kind to dragonswans, for thou art gorgeous when naked and taste good with Cool Whip."

What Dreams May Come

ALL-NEW STORIES OF MAGICAL ROMANCE

Knightly Dreams
by *New York Times* bestselling author
Sherrilyn Kenyon

Road to Adventure
by award-winning author
Robin D. Owens

Shattered Dreams
by *USA Today* bestselling author
Rebecca York

0-425-20268-2

Available wherever books are sold or at
penguin.com

b864

Four all–new stories of midnight fantasies.

Man of My Dreams

New York Times bestselling author
Maggie Shayne

USA Today bestselling author
Suzanne Forster

USA Today bestselling author
Virginia Kantra

New York Times bestselling author
Sherrilyn Kenyon

0–515–13793–6

Available wherever books are sold or at
penguin.com

Catch all the
Hot Shots

*Six quick reads from
six of your favorite bestselling authors!*

Magic in the Wind
by **Christine Feehan**
0-425-20863-X

Bridal Jitters by **Jayne Castle**
0-425-20864-8

Midnight in Death by **J.D. Robb**
0-425-20881-8

Spellbound by **Nora Roberts**
0-515-14077-5

Dragonswan by **Sherrilyn Kenyon**
0-515-14079-1

Immortality by **Maggie Shayne**
0-515-14078-3

Available wherever books are sold or at
penguin.com

J864